THIEVES

C. R. FULTON

Thieves
1st edition
Copyright © 2020 by C.R. Fulton & Bluewater Publications

BWPublications.com
Florence, Alabama

Library of Congress Control Number: 2020911901
ISBN - 978-1-949711-74-5 Paperback
ISBN - 978-1-949711-75-2 eBook

All rights reserved under International and Pan-American Copyright Convention. No part of this publication may be reproduced or transmitted in any form or by any means, electronic or mechanical, including photocopying, recording, or by any information storage and retrieval system, without prior written permission from the Publisher.

Published in the United States by Bluewater Publications.
BWPublications.com • Florence, Alabama

This work is based from the author's personal research and interpretation.

Managing Editor — Angela Broyles
Editor — Sierra Tabor
Interior Design — Rachel Davis
Cover Design — C. R. Fulton

DEDICATION

To all my "oily" people, because we love the same things! If you are reading this book, you probably love essential oils. I do too, and just to be fair to everyone, the company in this book is fictitious. I am sure you have a brand you love, so just go ahead and insert your beloved company's name and enjoy!

CHAPTER ONE

"Hurry up, Bugle!" My goldendoodle looks up at me, squinting in the cold rain. "Come on, girl. Get busy." She sneezes as she turns, finally squatting.

I shiver, resisting the breeze cutting through my sheer pantyhose. Blowing a cold raindrop off the tip of my nose, I wish I could wipe off my day at work as easily. I can't wait to hole up in my apartment with pajama pants, a cup of coffee, and some essential oil.

Normally, we'd take a walk at this time of day, but in this weather it's out of the question. To make up for the lack of exercise, I decide to take the three flights of stairs up to my apartment instead of the elevator. My stiletto heel catches in the third stair step. Bugle wasn't expecting my sudden halt, and she continues exuberantly bounding up the stairs. "Ahh!" Surprisingly, her hard yank on the leash is exactly what I need to pry my shoe off the metal weave in the staircase.

Bugle shakes the rain from her curly tan coat, and I'm instantly soaked. Sucking in a breath, I force everything away. Just make it to the door, that's all. Rounding the corner to the next flight, I shift forward so my heels won't get stuck again; my tight, knee-length skirt hampers my movement. Bugle stops suddenly in front of me. Her ever-wagging tail stills.

"What's up, girl? Let's go."

She answers with a low growl, sending shivers across my skin. Her strange behavior sets me on edge. Off-balance with my classy shoes, I edge around her before noticing a boot sticking out at the next landing. I come to a standstill as I consider the possibilities. Could be a drunk, hiding from the weather, passed out on the floor. The morning news flashes across my mind: another gang-related shooting in Raleigh. Bugle's sharp bark makes me jump, but the boot doesn't move. Maybe it's empty. Maybe one of my neighbors dropped it on their way down to work.

That's ridiculous since no empty footwear could stick out at that angle without a leg holding it up. I consider backing down, taking the elevator, and calling security. But the stillness draws me forward; I couldn't leave someone in need of help.

Dragging Bugle, I creep forward. "Aren't you supposed to protect me?" I whisper to my beloved pup. She growls again, prompting me to adjust my keys so three of them are sticking out between my fingers right near my knuckles. I could totally take somebody out. Right, Stephanie, sure you could.

Two more steps, then I gasp as I peer around the corner. "Richard!" The apartment manager's face, normally a pleasant ebony, has a pale gray tinge, and his glassy eyes stare up at the ceiling.

"Richard! Can you hear me?" I release Bugle's leash to as long as it will go as I kneel by my friend's side. Lifeguard training from high school surfaces, and I lift his limp arm, searching for a pulse. My stomach twists as the cold stillness confirms what my heart knew the instant I'd seen him. He's dead. Fighting sudden nausea, I stand, retreating toward Bugle and digging for my phone. My thumb trembles as I dial 911.

"9-1-1, what's your emergency?" The calm female voice is a polar opposite of mine.

"I . . . there's a . . . um . . . Richard's dead." Tears start to flow, twisting my voice. "I need . . . he needs help." I shake my head; my words won't go together correctly.

"Ma'am, what's your location?"

I draw a blank. "Um . . . I'm at my apartment. In the staircase."

"All right, ma'am, can you get me the address?"

Come on Stephanie, get it together. "Yes." Still, it takes me a moment to think of it, but then I am able to rattle off the apartment's address without stuttering.

"Excellent. An officer is on his way, ma'am. Can I get your name?" I wish her self-control would rub off on me.

"My name is Stephanie Pierce. I was just coming home from work." My voice rises, threatening to break on the last word.

"Yes, ma'am. You said the man's first name is Richard?"

I clear my throat. "Yes, Richard. Richard Hubbler. He's the apartment manager. He is—was—a wonderful man. I've lived here three years, and he's been great to deal with. So helpful."

"And you said he's dead? Are you certain, Stephanie?"

I nod. "My first job was as a lifeguard. I checked his pulse; there's nothing. He's cold." My hand presses against my throat as Bugle leans on my legs, trembling. We are a mess. I sniff my dripping nose and wipe my eyes.

"All right, ma'am. Help is about two minutes out. Just hang tight. Is there anyone else present?"

Her question makes me press back against the wall. I glance up and down the hall, hating that my voice sinks to a whisper. "I don't think so." Bugle whines, staring up at me through her blonde bangs. "Shhhh," I say as I stroke her head.

"Who are you talking to, Stephanie?" The operator questions.

"Oh, my dog. She's really upset. She knew he was there way before I did."

"Okay, an officer is in the parking lot. What end of the building are you on?"

"Drive all the way around to the left. It's the rear staircase, near the grass," I say.

8

"Got it. Thank you, Stephanie. You should be seeing the officer any second."

"Yes, I hear him," I respond, hearing the echo of footsteps. Bugle's tail thumps my thigh. She sure likes live people better than dead ones. My stomach twists at the thought.

"Excellent. He will help you from here, Stephanie."

"Oh," I reply. No part of me wants to be doing this.

"I'm going to hang up now; the officer will help you."

I wish I had taken the elevator.

"Oh." I don't want to make the switch. I like my super-calm phone operator.

"Goodbye." Click.

And just like that, I'm cut off. A shadow precedes the officer up the staircase, and Bugle's whole body begins to wag. I feel limp, like a wet rag, and find my mouth hanging open as a tall, wide-shouldered policeman clips up the stairs as if they are flat ground. Couldn't be more opposite than me, with my high heels sticking. I snap my mouth shut.

I lean back farther as Bugle strains toward the man in a light-blue uniform. His dark, close-cropped hair still tries to curl, and his brooding brown eyes scan me quickly. What does he see? A mess most likely. Still, his hand reaches down to ruffle Bugle's still wet fur. No ring on his left hand, I notice.

"Ma'am, I'm Officer Wellborn. You've got a body here?" I open my mouth to reply, but my words are all jumbled, so instead I point up the stairwell.

He springs up the steps. As he squeezes past, I can't help noticing how his short sleeves are stretched taut by muscle. His faint, masculine cologne lingers as he disappears around the landing. A few seconds pass in silence, then his radio crackles. His deep voice is drowned out by the noise of more footsteps pounding up the stairs.

Three EMT paramedics huff up the stairs. I point woodenly at the landing, struggling to hold Bugle back. I feel as if I've been standing in a pounding black-flag surf at Atlantic Beach. I suck in a breath, trying to pull myself together before Officer Wellborn reappears.

A second later I hear, "You're Stephanie, right?" He's so tall, two stairs above me. I try not to shrink back.

"Yes, sir," I manage to answer.

"Let's get out of this stairwell; I'll need to take a statement from you. Can we head down and take the elevator?"

"Mm-hmm." I nod, staring down at the stairs that want to eat my shoes. An EMT rushes past, love handles jiggling as he descends. Bugle yanks the leash hard; she's had enough of this tight space. Me too. Her exuberance plus my rubbery legs force me to reach out for the railing.

Officer Wellborn squeezes past and starts down. Did he just go ahead of me to be sure I won't fall headlong? My grandfather always did that for my grandmother when going down the stairs. The sweet memories bring me back to myself. Taking a deep breath, I try bending my knees so my heels won't jam into the millions of evil holes.

On the next landing, the EMT nearly knocks me in the head with the stretcher as he navigates back up the stairs. Officer Wellborn's hand shoots out just in time, saving me from a nasty bruise. "Jim! Slow down, man."

The chubby EMT's face flushes red, then he's gone. Three more officers climb the stairs, and we wait on the landing for them to pass.

"Brandon, Casey, construct a timeline. Bobby, get this crime scene cordoned off." They nod in unison and continue. Crime scene? The blood drains out of my face. I hadn't seen anything that looked like a crime.

Officer Wellborn starts down the staircase, but since I don't follow, he turns back to look at me, now eye level. "Ready?" I stare into his handsome face with stubble barely starting to show and say nothing.

Can you look any more like a nincompoop, Steph? I force a timid smile. "Yes." Following his broad shoulders, I try not to let the crime scene thing get to me.

And then it happens. Clunk. Two steps from the bottom, my right heel sinks deep into the stair as Bugle leaps the last step. She hits the end of the leash, but I'm anchored solidly to the building so her motion forces my arm to thwack Officer Wellborn hard in the shoulder. He spins, lightning fast, his hand closing like a vice on my wrist before he sees I'm not attacking, that it was Bugle.

"I'm so sorry! Oh!"

Bugle sees the grass and yanks hard again. The officer lets me go, and his hands spread wide in front of him.

"I'm sorry, ma'am. Are you all right?"

"I'm . . . well," I try to yank my heel loose, but it won't budge. I bite my lip as I say sheepishly, "My shoe seems to be stuck."

His brow furrows in confusion until I bend sideways and struggle with my shoe.

"Here, let me help you." He leans down, breath tickling my ear as I stand up. There's not enough space for both of us. He shoves a thick finger between the metal step and the sole of my shoe and yanks. Nothing.

"Wow! You do seem to be stuck. Uh, let me try . . ." Repositioning, he tries to help without touching my legs. Finally, he straightens.

"You're going to have to take it off, ma'am."

I nod. Sure, why not? It fits the day perfectly. After what feels like an eternity, the clasp on my shoe slips loose, and my foot slides free. I'm back on solid ground, again wishing I had just taken the elevator.

Officer Wellborn wrestles with my super-cute stiletto. Eventually, it twists free, and his mouth pulls sideways as he inspects the ruined leather.

"I think it's done for." He holds it up; it looks small in his hand.

I reach out for it. "I don't think I ever want to see these shoes again." Unstrapping the other one, I find they make an incredibly satisfying clunk in the garbage can at the base of the stairs. He looks even taller and more imposing without my heels.

As we step into the elevator, he pulls out a notebook. "All right, full name please."

"Stephanie Joy Pierce." He scribbles a lot longer than it could possibly take to write those three words. I imagine his list—Caucasian, 5'5" female; mid-length, damp, stringy brown hair; mascara running past teary blue eyes; prone to accidents; not very good at speaking. The elevator doors swish open and, voilà, just like that, I have finally arrived on the third floor of Circle Court Apartments—with no shoes and a male escort. Bugle pulls me toward our door to the right, wanting her treat.

"I'm going to need you to give me a bit more info before you go, ma'am." I nod, longing for pajama pants.

"Where do you work, and what's your position?"

At least that's something I can talk about. "I'm an executive assistant to Harry Thorn at Blue Stone Enterprises."

He nods. "Down on Main Street?"

"Yes."

"Great. Do you get home about this time every day?" he questions.

"That's correct. I go pick up Bugle at daycare and then get home about now."

"Bugle?" The strange name confuses him, and I can see him wondering if I've left a kid in my car.

I reach down and stroke Bugle's ears. "When I got her as a pup, she had one big curl on the top of her head; it looked just like a Bugle chip. The curl stayed the same size as she grew." I shrug my shoulders as I flatten all her other fluff, showcasing her namesake in the center of her forehead.

"I see it now."

This poor guy is just trying to investigate a "crime scene," and here I am showing off my dog's intense cuteness. I straighten. "What else do you need to know?"

"What kind of car do you drive, ma'am?" His pen is ready to record my answer.

"A silver Accord. 2018."

"License plate?"

I screw up one side of my nose; apparently, that's answer enough.

"It's all right. I'll find it later. How long have you known Richard?"

His question makes me think. Tears rise along with the image of Richard's ashen face. "Three years? He runs the apartment complex. I just can't say enough about him. He was a great guy." I press my fingers to my forehead. "Oh, I'll have to tell Bonita. They've been married thirty-five years." My throat tightens.

"We'll take care of it." His voice is quiet.

"Officer Wellborn, do you really think he was murdered?" I question.

He softens just a bit. "It's procedure to treat all bodies as a homicide at first. But to be honest, I didn't see any sign of struggle—could just be natural causes. Did he have anyone in the building that he didn't get along with?"

"Well, no," I answer before adding, "Maybe you could check the guy at the end of the hall."

"Name?" He looks down the hall in the direction I point.

"Oh . . . um." I roll my eyes up to the left. "Sam! His first name is Sam. That's all I know. He's been late on his rent a few times." I look up to find dark eyes studying my face.

"Call me Mark. Let me get your number, and I'll be in contact."

I nod, rattling off my number. "I will only be here for another ten days though," I add, thinking of my schedule.

His dark brow goes up. "Vacation?"

"No, I travel for work. I spend two weeks here and two weeks at my condo in Salt Lake City. That's why Bugle goes to doggie daycare. She's happy staying there when I'm out of state."

Mark scribbles on his notepad again. Then he reaches out to pet Bugle. "See you, Bugle. Miss Pierce, I'll keep you posted."

"Thanks," I respond, but he doesn't move. Finally, it clicks. He's waiting to be sure I get in my apartment safely.

THIEVES

I fumble with my keys. Bugle rushes in, happy as ever, and I turn, watching the handsome officer till the door clicks shut, and he disappears from my sight.

CHAPTER TWO

"Richard's dead?" My best friend's voice is pinched. "And you found the body? Girl, that's a rough day."

Beck gets me. We are as opposite as we can be— she's my crazy, and I'm her normal.

"Did you puke?" she asks.

"Nope, I was pretty chill. Except my stiletto heel kept getting stuck in the stairs, and the last time it did, the officer had to pull it out."

Beck's loud laugh makes me smile for the first time today. "All that calls for a girls' night out. You know those essential oil classes you've been trying to get me to come to forever? Well, tonight's the night."

She always springs things on me at the last second. Usually it's a movie she wants to go to, and she expects me to make it spur of the moment. It's hardly ever an issue since my social calendar is disappointingly empty. Hers is full of dates with more guys than I've met in the last year. Still, I'm thrilled she's coming.

She doesn't hesitate. "I'll pick you up at 6:30. Don't take the stairs." Silence.

She's hung up on me, leaving me no room to back out.

I look up as Harry barrels into my office. "Get Fairbanks Commodities on line one. Did you force that no-good lawyer to get me my subpoena?"

Harry Thorn is an incredibly difficult man. Because he stands six foot four, everybody looks up to him whether or not they want to. When his brown eyes are darker than normal like right now, you've got to be on your toes. I slide a dark blue folder off my desk; he snatches it out of my hand.

"I will need a list of gravel composition by noon along with shipping costs. Call Chimera's and get me a table for three at five o'clock. Contact all the invites for the meeting in Utah to make sure they're coming."

His lip pulls up in a sneer. "Then call that new secretary in here and fire her. She's not the caliber I need. Find a new one; make sure she's blonde." Harry turns on his heel without another word.

Sure, Harry, sure. I'll get all that. It's only a list that could fill three days, and I've got till noon. I open my lavender oil and inhale. I sigh, jotting "Schedule suit fitting before Friday" at the end of my list. It's my job to keep him looking sharp.

Beck's red Mustang pulls up exactly ten minutes late. "You're early," I say.

She grins. "I know it! I'm really making some changes—used to always be at least twenty minutes late." I barely shut my door before she floors it. I glance at her. She's heavyset but carries the weight well, her dark, shining hair somehow always perfectly curled.

"So, you know where we are going?" I question.

"You texted me the address, remember? How was work?"

I sigh because work has escalated into a whirlwind of stress.

"Harry is going through with the lawsuit. So, I'll have somewhere around three extra hours of work every day, hunting down the paperwork attorneys want. But, of course, I won't get paid any extra for it. Plus, we've got that merger in Utah. I don't see how I'm going to get through it." We exit the thruway toward the residential end of town.

"I think I forgot to eat dinner." Beck's used to my weird food habits.

"Maybe you should quit. You're worth far more than Harry pays you. Plus, he doesn't have the right to treat you like dirt."

I grunt, agreeing with the last comment. "If I could find another job that would pay what Harry

19

does, I would. But I really want to own a house free and clear by the time I'm thirty."

Beck gives a low whistle. "Eight years doesn't leave you much time."

"I'll make it." I nod to myself. That's why I'm going to start doing Essential Sense oils as a business. Then I shake my head. "Couldn't find my keys today though."

Beck looks at me horrified. "I'm the one who misplaces stuff. You never do. What's going on? Finding the body really got to you, huh?"

I nod. "Yeah. I just can't seem to get Richard's face out of my mind. I wish I knew if it was foul play. Can't imagine anyone wanting to hurt him." I feel like the words come out in slow motion, the driver of an oncoming white van with no windows in the back stares hard at me as we pass. I swallow hard, mouth suddenly dry.

Beck's GPS interrupts, "You have arrived." I look around to see we've arrived in a neighborhood of unfamiliar houses.

"We've arrived?" I crinkle my nose, returning to reality. "I thought Sheena's house was yellow."

Beck grins. "GPS could be wrong. I say we knock anyway and see what we find." A bunch of cars are parked around the blue house we're in front of. She rummages through her console and smacks a pack of trail mix in my lap. "Let's go." She's out of the car and up the sidewalk before I haul myself out, stuffing in a mouthful of nuts.

"Welcome! Come on in, Steph. Who's your friend?"

I step up to the door and shake the pretty blonde woman's hand. "This is my best friend, Beck." As I step into the house, I'm enveloped by a scent I have come to deeply love. It's a large, deep smell, but somehow peaceful too. The aroma of essential oils.

"I'm Sheena. I'm so glad you're here, Beck! Come on in and sit down."

I follow Beck to an empty two-seater sofa. As I sink into it, I'm suddenly back in the stairwell. Richard's glassy eyes are staring up out of his ashen face. I rub my forehead, trying to wipe away the image. This is at least the seventh time that such an intense memory has gripped me, and it seems to be totally uncontrollable. It's just not okay to be preoccupied like that, especially at work. I focus on the present. Sheena is the lady who introduced me to oils a few years ago.

"Welcome everyone! I'm Sheena, and I'm happy you came tonight. We are here to learn about something that changed my life. Essential oils! How many of you just thought, essential what?" Sheena raises her hand, and five or six of the other ladies raise theirs as well.

"Well, three years ago I was not doing well physically. My brain always seemed foggy; I didn't have enough energy to keep up with the day—much less have any energy left for things that I really enjoyed. My doctor said what I was experiencing was just part of getting older, but at thirty-six, that explanation just couldn't be right! My grandmother was 89, and she was in better shape than I was. My skin was dry, my hair was dull, and I was getting so many wrinkles!

"So, that's when I did exactly what you're doing tonight. I went to a friend's house and attended a 'class' she was holding. I went because it seemed as if she had the things I was longing for: energy, focus, and vibrant skin, even though she was older than me. I'm glad to tell you she convinced me to make a few changes, and those changes made all the difference. How many of you feel as if you could use more energy and focus?"

Every hand in the room goes up in answer to her question.

"Great! Let's take a look at some issues that are causing you to feel as if you're deficient in those areas. Did you know that the average American woman puts over three hundred chemicals on her skin every day? Eighty of those are usually before breakfast. 'Chemicals?' you ask. Yes, they are disguised as personal care products, cleaners, laundry detergent and even . . .'" Sheena makes a horrified face. "Scented candles. Yes, ladies, scented candles and plug-ins are listed as the most toxic and deadly items in your home. Did you hear that? Burning a scented candle for a mere half an hour is as carcinogenic as smoking an entire cigarette. Plus, the wick emits lead. How about your kids and pets? Would you want them to be exposed to a room full of cigarette smoke? And yet, without knowing it, every time we burn a scented candle, that's exactly what we're doing!"

I think about the pumpkin spice candles I used to love, but now it's my diffuser I turn to.

"Let's consider laundry detergent for a minute. How many hours per day is it on your skin? Okay!" She holds up her hands. "I don't want you to answer out loud just in case!"

All the ladies chuckle.

"But I would dare to say that most of us have laundry detergent against our skin almost constantly. We wear it, we sleep in it, and we wrap our babies in it."

I think of Bugle at home curled up on her freshly laundered bed. I used to spray it with Febreze.

Sheena continues, "Laundry detergent is loaded with carcinogens that are snug against our skin almost twenty-four hours a day, seven days a week. Then I learned more. Do we have any ER nurses here in this room?"

Two women raise their hands.

"Great, so what do y'all do when you have a patient come in who is in cardiac arrest? What's the fastest way to bring them out of it?" Sheena asks.

A dark-haired woman responds, "We would give them a nitrous oxide pill."

Sheena nods. "Yep, and how would you administer that drug?" she questions.

The nurse responds, "We would put it under the person's tongue."

"Why there?" Sheena responds with a sparkle in her eye. She loves this interaction, and I enjoy listening and watching simply because of her passion.

The nurse shrugs her shoulders. "Because it's the fastest way to get the drug directly into the bloodstream; it's the fastest absorption point in the body."

Sheena nods, building suspense. "Hearing this fact got me to thinking. Everything that goes under my tongue gets absorbed directly into my bloodstream. I went home and flipped over my tube of toothpaste. Amid the incredibly long list of chemicals I couldn't pronounce was one that I was familiar with: sodium lauryl sulfate—a proven carcinogen. Proven. And that's what I've been absorbing directly into my bloodstream twice a day for the last thirty-nine years!"

Sheena does not look thirty-nine years old. I would've guessed maybe thirty.

"I threw that toothpaste in the trash can immediately. My mouthwash too; its ingredients were even worse. But I had to have something! I didn't want a stinky house, dirty clothes, and crusty teeth! Thankfully, that's when I sat in someone's living room just like this and learned about essential oils. They have replaced every chemical in my life—not just any essential oils either—Essential Sense! I'm going to pass around some for you to smell. First, I'm going to pass a bottle of department store peppermint and then a bottle of Essential Sense peppermint. Smell the generic brand first and then the Essential Sense."

Beck sniffs the department-store brand and hands it to me. The odor makes me think of Christmas and peppermint mocha. I lean way out to hand it to the next lady. Beck's eyes snap open wide as she smells the Essential Sense peppermint. I smile, remembering the first time I'd smelled it. I inhale long and low. My nose tingles as my throat clears; it's so strong it almost makes my eyes water. Ah.

"Beck, what difference did you notice between the two oils?" Sheena asks.

"Well, the first oil smelled like a candy cane. I thought it was pretty strong until I smelled the Essential Sense! Actually, now that I think about it, the first one smelled more like alcohol, and the Essential Sense is like pure peppermint."

"Exactly. Even though the generic does say "100% pure therapeutic grade," the FDA rules only require companies to add five percent essential oil in that bottle with this labeling. The scary thought is they are not required at all to label the other ingredients in ninety-five percent of the bottle! That's why I love and trust Essential Sense. Their homegrown guarantee pledges one hundred percent pure oil. Next, I'm going to pass along an oil blend called Relax."

In a moment, the bottle of Relax is under my nose. At first, I notice vanilla and lime. Then the most amazing thing happens. It feels like a spring that's been wound way too tight is loosening deep inside me. I breathe out, and my shoulders drop as memories of Richard in the stairwell fade away. I feel okay, balanced. I inhale again and close my eyes this time.

Beck elbows me in the ribs and whispers, "You're supposed to pass it along, Steph."

I keep my eyes closed. "I can't." I can sense Beck staring at me, but I'm not ready to part with the little green bottle.

"Ahh. Let me get another bottle to pass around," I hear Sheena say. "Happens almost every time. Someone just can't let it go. You just go ahead and hug it, Stephanie."

"Thank you," I respond. And that's how I stay for I don't know how long. It's as if layer after layer of inner tightness unlocks. I ran out of Relax almost a month ago. Sheena continues speaking, but I don't really hear her. It's just me and the scent of the oils.

My ears perk up at her next question.

"So, who's ready to change her life with an Essential Sense starter kit?"

Beck's hand shoots into the air. I am already a believer.

"Great, Beck! Since your hand went up first, go ahead and take a bottle of Superberry home with you; it's a super-power, all-natural, energy drink. Get on your phone and type in 'Essential Sense.' Go to the main website and click on 'become a member!'"

I'm still floating on the absence of tension inside when Beck shows me her phone: "Congratulations on becoming an Essential Sense member."

Beck whispers, "We're staying for the business training. I have to know more."

My belly growls, but I had been planning on it.

Beck is ecstatic when we get in her car. "I am so excited to get started! Open my kit!" Sheena had one flip kit with her. Meaning that Beck was the only one to get her kit tonight. Everyone else will get theirs in the mail.

The huge Essential Sense box barely fits on my lap, but I rip it open, revealing all the beautiful oils. I look over at Beck. "Thanks for coming with me."

She shrugs. "All these years you've been right. I needed this."

TUESDAY, 5:45 A.M.

My phone rings just as I am about to head out the door for work. Who would call this early? I gulp down my last sip of coffee.

"Hello?" My voice comes out a bit peeved.

"Hello, Miss Pierce. This is Officer Wellborn. I need you to sign some additional statements this morning. I was hoping to catch you before you left for work."

I draw a breath. The to-do list for Harry is longer than ever. But if a law enforcement officer asks you to do something, you have to do it, right?

"This morning?" I question, hoping for a way out.

"Yes, ma'am." His deep baritone leaves no room for argument. "I can call your boss and tell him you'll be late. The police station is on your way to work; it shouldn't take you too much extra time."

I grit my teeth, dreading Harry's wrath. "All right. What time?" I snatch my bottle of Relax off the counter; Sheena had given it to me after hearing about me finding Richard.

"Would twenty minutes from now be good?"

"Sure," I find myself agreeing. "Do I go to the front desk?"

"Yes, ma'am. I'll meet you there."

I shiver even in the warm morning on the small grassy yard as I wait to scoop up Bugle's waste, wondering how long Richard's death will be an unforeseen chapter of my life. We haven't taken the stairs since. Sam trots down the stairs, the metallic sound sending shivers down my spine. He halts on seeing me, drops his eyes, and cuts around the building as quickly as possible. He looks guilty. I look down to find my hand white knuckled around Bugle's leash. I force a deep breath.

"Come on, Bugle. Let's go talk to the cops." Bugle wags her tail hard, expecting to go to daycare. "Sorry, girl. You'll have to wait in the car." I hate the thought though. What if she gets too hot?

Halfway to the station, a text bleeps in. "Bring Bugle in with you. No point in getting a misdemeanor for animal cruelty. – Mark."

I almost smile; really, he seems to know everything. I try to relax my shoulders. Why can't I just have my quiet, private life back? I grab my purse and rub a drop of Citrus Essence oil under my jawline. Too soon we're at the station, and I'm clipping on Bugle's leash, with butterflies in my stomach. It's just because of the situation, but I still double-check my hair before leaving the car.

"Let's get this over with, girl." I straighten my tight, knee-length skirt, thankful for my sturdy mid-height heels today. Bugle's nails click on the atrium's tile floor. There, leaning against the front desk, Officer Wellborn is laughing at something the secretary said. His thick arms are crossed over his chest and remembering how his muscles had rippled as he freed my stiletto from the staircase comes back in a rush. I take a deep breath, trying not to notice the hint of dark stubble over his square jaw.

He straightens when he catches sight of Bugle and me. Bugle starts to wiggle as Officer Wellborn squats down to greet her. This time I manage a real smile as he and the secretary make a fuss over my fur baby.

"Miss Pierce, come on back to my office," he says, standing with his arm outstretched. I nod and fall into step beside him. Bugle sticks her nose into every open doorway till we enter a huge room full of cubicles. Bugle is a mess of wiggles from the hands reaching out to pet her as we weave through the labyrinth of desks. Mark's wide arm guides me into a spare cube, just a desk and some chairs, no personal effects.

"Please have a seat, Miss Pierce."

"You can call me Stephanie." I clear my throat. "Do you know why Richard died?"

He nods, and his deep brown eyes catch mine, "Richard was a diabetic. He died of hypoglycemia."

Perplexed, I shake my head in consternation. "That's so strange; Richard never seemed to be weak. He worked hard all day every day. And he certainly never mentioned having diabetes."

Officer Wellborn doesn't reply except to push the papers across the desk and tap the bottom of the sheet. "This is a witness statement; if you would, please sign it on the line provided at the bottom." He slides the pen across the desk with his free hand.

"Bugle, sit." She licks her chops as she obeys, and I squiggle my signature.

"So, what can you tell me about Sam Hanover?" he asks.

"Sam?" I say to buy time. What should I say? That he looked guilty?

"Sam, the guy down the hall in apartment 315." Officer Wellborn leans back in his chair, his arms once again crossed over his chest, badge catching the light. Nothing glimmers on his left hand. Of course, he might wear a wedding band when he's off duty. I feel the color rise in my face; I sure hope he doesn't think it's because of Sam.

"He never talks to me. Every time he sees me, he heads the other way. He doesn't seem to work though. No schedule that I can tell anyway." I shrug.

Mark grunts, "He's extremely allergic to dogs, so that's probably why he avoids you and your pup."

I nod. "Seems as if you know more about him than I do. I saw him this morning." I think back to his perfect knowledge of my schedule. Why would he still be digging if he thought Richard had died of natural causes? I lean forward. "Officer Wellborn, did you seriously call my boss?"

"It's Mark, remember? And yes, I didn't want you to be late on my account when I could put in an official word for you." He smiles.

"Thanks. Was he rude?" I can't help asking.

Mark's voice is flat. "I wasn't impressed. I'll leave it at that. Does he treat you that way?"

I smile, brushing it off. "Every day."

Mark pushes back his chair, towering on the far side of the desk. "Well, thanks for coming in. I don't want to hold you up and risk Harry's wrath."

"Oh, I can handle him. Do you know when Richard's funeral is?" I ask as I look up at him.

"I don't believe a date has been set yet. Still some paperwork to clear him for burial."

I nod as I stand. "Come on, Bugle."

Mark heads for the main door, and I find myself staring at the back of his thick neck and the impressive width of his shoulders. I bump into the corner of a desk as we near the exit. Get it together, Steph. He steps into the doorway first, but Bugle has other ideas. She yanks, leaping ahead into the lobby. She tows me like a skier so that Mark and I are squeezed into the doorframe together. My free hand comes up seeking balance and finds Mark's chest. He catches my elbow in one hand and the leash in the other.

"You all right?" he asks.

My mouth opens, but nothing will come out. I haven't stood this close to a man in a very long time. I stare at him like a deer in the headlights. He seems perfectly content as he takes in the details of my face. Finally, I rein in my senses.

"Oh, sorry." I slip out of the tight doorway and head down the hall, face bright red. Bugle, how could you?

In the car, I rub on a drop of Germ Sniper hand sanitizer, and the invigorating scent fills the cabin. By the time I pull into daycare, I'm ready to go home, but the day's not even begun. Bugle trembles with excitement as we walk through the door.

"Stephanie! You're late." The front desk guy's name is Jerome, and his mocha skin and bright brown eyes match his concerned tone.

"I know! I had to go to the police station."

Bugle leaps into Jerome's arms; it's their thing. Every morning she jumps into Jerome's lanky embrace and licks his face.

"What?" He turns his head, trying to talk and keep Bugle from licking his mouth. "Do they know anything more about the dead man?" he questions.

"No, not really. I guess he died from diabetes." I shrug sadly.

Jerome nods as his short dreadlocks bob. "Bugle, you smell good, but you don't get your bath till Thursday."

I jump in at Jerome's comment, ready to start telling people about how much oils have helped me. "It's an oil," I say.

"Oil?" Jerome's nose crinkles up in question.

"Yeah, essential oil. It's what gives plants their immunity to disease. They're awesome."

Jerome nods, setting down my wiggling dog. "Well, it sure smells nice."

I want to pour out more of my oil knowledge, but I'm late. If I get any later, I may have to put some Relax on Harry.

TUESDAY, 7:45 P.M.

Curled up on my couch with Bugle snuggled next to me, I look at my phone and see that it's Beck. I smile as I answer. "Hey!"

"Sold two kits today," she announces. Beck never says hello.

"What?! That's awesome!" I think that's good for me too. Sheena said Beck was on my "team."

"Yep. How was your day?"

I sigh as I think about how to answer. "Well, I was way late to work, and Harry made me pay for it."

"Excuse me, but did you say you were late for work?" Her incredulous tone says it all. I am never late.

"Mark called and said I had to sign some papers." I bite my lip, thinking of the morning.

"Mark?" Her voice is flat.

"Yeah, you know, the cute officer?" I say without thinking.

There's a perfect silence on the other end before her exclamation. "Did you say cute?"

Well, I can't back out of it now. I'll just have to own it. "Yep."

"I'm coming over." She hangs up.

If I know her, she'll be here in ten minutes with ice cream.

Sure enough, Bugle barks at the doorbell ringing twelve minutes later. Beck passes me a tub of triple chocolate.

"I'm going to put some peppermint oil in this ice cream, and then you're going to spill." My blunt friend Beck.

"Make mine a big bowl," I say. The smell of the peppermint oil fills the room as Beck chops it into the ice cream, then she adds a few drops to the lemon oil I already had in my diffuser. Didn't take her long to become an oiler.

She licks her spoon and rolls her eyes. "Oh, it's way better than I thought it would be."

We plop on the couch. Beck is one of those heavyset women who should really be a model because even though she's not thin, she's beautiful.

"Okay, tell me about the cuteness, 'cause I haven't heard you say anything like that since that jerk Jim left you five years ago. Thank God!" She digs into her ice cream as she waits for me to begin explaining.

I shrug. "He was the first one on the scene when I found Richard. Wellborn. Remember? Oh, the ice cream is good. He rescued my shoe?"

"Mmm." I can't tell if she's moaning about the excellence of the peppermint and chocolate or saying that she remembers.

"Well, he called this morning saying I needed to sign some papers before work." I smile. "He even called Harry and told him I was going to be late due to official business. Who thinks of things like that?"

"Well, if he survived a phone call with Harry, he must be tough," she says.

"Right?" I agree. "He is tough, big muscles too."

"Touching? There was touching too?!" Beck sits forward in anticipation.

I roll my eyes. "Not on purpose. Bugle pulled me through the doorway as he was walking through." I can't contain a giggle.

She looks at Bugle. "I always knew there was something special about you, Buge." She glances up at me. "He's not married, is he?"

"I don't know. He doesn't wear a ring at work at least."

Beck's eyes gleam. "Let's find out." She whips out her phone. "Ha! They still haven't found those diamonds from McMurray's yet," she says, skimming the headlines.

I grunt; a million dollars' worth of diamonds had been stolen in Raleigh two months ago without a trace.

"W-E-L-L-B-O-R-N."

There she goes. She belongs to some site that knows everything about everybody.

"Six-foot-two, twenty-five years old, two hundred twenty pounds. Oohhh. He is cute—really cute. He has to be married, Steph. Guys like that don't hang around on the market for long. But no . . . he's never been married. Well, what's wrong with him then?" Suddenly Beck's mouth drops open as her eyes scan back and forth across her phone.

My spoon stops halfway to my mouth. "What?" I question.

"Oh!" is all she says.

"What?" I demand again.

She sighs. "He was engaged four years ago. Two weeks before the wedding, his fiancée was killed. Vehicular manslaughter charges were brought against the other driver. Poor guy. So, he lives in Raleigh; his mom lives here too. Volunteers as a football coach. Can this guy get any more lovable?"

My ice cream plops off the spoon as I consider all he's gone through.

"Drives a nice truck though. My favorite color." Beck keeps hunting. "Favorite fast food is Wendy's. He's the youngest of two sons. The older brother David lives in Oregon. His father passed away two years ago."

"You give me the creeps when you find stuff like that. What happened to privacy?" I say, scraping the bottom of my bowl.

"Privacy is dead. Will you get me more? Three drops of peppermint please." She holds up her empty bowl.

"Sure," I say as I take our bowls back for a refill.

"Hey, did you sign up for the Essential Bonus yet?" Beck's question pulls me from deep thoughts on the information about Mark.

"Yeah, I did a few months ago. It's a monthly order program with Essential Sense. You get points and tons of free stuff."

Beck rolls her eyes. "I know what it is. I'm signing up now." She's a consummate shopper, and when she finds a good deal, she sticks with it. "Hey! There's a little purple star by my name, Stephanie! I ranked up to Star."

I hand over her bowl of ice cream and lean in to look. Sure enough, there's a pretty purple star by her name in her Essential Sense virtual office.

"Sweet," I respond.

"Did you order Superberry yet?" she asks.

I nod. "It's one of the most incredible substances you can put in your body. More antioxidants than you can imagine. Oh, will you please log into my account and order me foundation, blush, and eyeshadow? You're better at picking colors than I am."

She looks back at her phone. "Sure! What's your password? I'll put it on your Essential Bonus order." A few minutes later, she says, "Okay. I've spent some of your mountains of money. Your makeup should be here in two days."

"Thanks," I say.

Beck heads home, and I start my nightly routine. Stepping into the bathroom, I stare hard at the sink. The bottle of Relax is turned just a bit. I always line things up straight. My chest tightens. Had Beck used the bathroom while she was here? No, I am sure she didn't. Must have been Bugle. I shake my head. She doesn't jump on things. Plus, wouldn't she have knocked them over, not turned them around?

I bite my lip, peering down the dark hallway. Calm down, Stephanie. You're off your game lately. I must have left the bottle that way. Still, before bed, Bugle and I make a careful inspection of the apartment.

CHAPTER THREE

Cleaning is my thing. Peaceful, normal. I've vacuumed, dusted; now it's time to scrub the sinks. I flip my normal cleaner over and read the warning list. Sheena's words are fresh in my mind. Maybe not. I Google essential oil cleaner recipe. I see I need to buy some Germ Sniper Home Defense. Till then I'll try the baking soda and Germ Sniper oil. Pleasantly surprised by its effectiveness, I try it on the shower too. I've got music playing, and Bugle and I are deep in a game of tug when I barely hear a knock at the door.

"Some guard dog you are." Bugle's bright brown eyes follow the rope toy as I whip it down the hall. Peering through the peephole, I hiss under my breath. My handsome officer stands in the hall in his glamour pose with his arms across his chest. The apartment is a mess. I'm a mess. Finally, Bugle barks. Probably caught his scent under the door.

"SSHHH," I scold her to no avail. He knows I'm here now. Who am I kidding? He knows everything; of course, he knows I'm here.

"Um," I stutter. I will NOT open the door in sweatpants. "Hold on!" I shout, rocketing down the hall and stripping off my t-shirt. I drop the sweatpants in the middle of the bedroom floor. In seconds, I'm shrugging into skinny jeans and a sweater. I veer into the bathroom and grab the first bottle I find. Lemon. I rub it on and pull out my hairband. I grit my teeth as I think about the disaster of my apartment; I'm so not done cleaning yet. Letting out a deep breath, I nonchalantly open the door.

"Hey, Mark." Wow! I actually sound normal.

"Good afternoon. May I come in for a minute?"

I nod, stepping back as Bugle pushes past to greet him and he kneels to pet her.

He looks up at me as Bugle wiggles in a circle, soaking up the love. "How was your day, Stephanie?"

"Well . . ." I put my hand on my hip. "Work is done, so now I'm good." Mark grunts as he steps into my home. "How about you, Mark?"

He shrugs. "It's been an interesting day. Which," he sighs, "brought me here."

"Oh," I respond, wondering if that's such a bad thing.

"Not that I mind coming," He backpedals, catching my hesitation. "It's just the news I'm not looking forward to telling you."

"Oh," I say again, even more quietly, wishing a different word would come out of my mouth.

"Can we sit?" he questions.

"Of course. Would you like something to drink?" I ask as we move toward the couch.

"No, I'm good for now." He sits on the edge of the couch, one hand on Bugle's head and the other spread wide and beckoning me to sit.

I do so, wondering what he'll say.

"So, I told you at the station that Richard died of natural causes. The autopsy report came back as hypoglycemia as the cause of death, but I had a gut feeling that something wasn't right. I got permission to dig into his medical records. He was a type II diabetic, but he was only in the beginning stages, and the numbers on the autopsy don't match up to someone like Richard who was only on a super-low dose of insulin. My dad passed away from diabetes complications, so I know a good bit about the illness."

Two years ago. I feel bad knowing that information.

"Richard couldn't have progressed that fast. It was enough to get them to run some more labs. Turns out there's never been a case of death from as high an insulin level as Richard had."

My stomach drops as he talks. So, it was murder then? But the words won't come.

"The coroner found the injection site on his back. People don't give themselves insulin shots in the lower back. Anyway, I'll spare you the rest of the details, but your landlord's death has officially become a homicide case."

I feel my face go white, and I sink back against the couch. Mark jumps up and heads into my kitchen. I hear cupboard doors opening and then the clink of a glass.

The room starts to spin. I motion weakly. "Peppermint. Bottle. Tiny." That's all I can get out. I sure hope he can decipher my cryptic message.

A second later he's pressing a glass of water into my hand. He frowns at the tiny bottle of peppermint then cracks it open. "Whoa." His eyes are open wide now.

I take the bottle, passing it under my nose. Instantly the queasy feeling fades, and I take a sip of water.

"You better?" he questions, the couch tilting his way as he settles next to me.

"Mmhmm. I think so."

"That's one serious bottle of peppermint. The smell is still in my nose."

I smile. "Thanks for decoding my mumble."

"It's a skill of mine." As he smiles back at me, the angle of his jaw catches my attention, and I can't stop staring at him.

He bursts my bubble with his next words. "So, I wanted to let you know that there will be a few extra policemen around. You might see them here or at work. You might not see them, but they'll be within shouting distance." He snatches my phone off the coffee table and offers it to me to unlock it with my fingerprint. As I do, I think about how comfortable it is to have him on my couch and tinkering with my phone.

A few seconds later, a serious-looking icon of his face appears in my contact list. "If you need anything, call me."

I nod, taking back my phone and looking at the new icon. "It's a nice picture." Did that just come out of my mouth?

A slow grin spreads across his face. "Thanks."

My stomach drops again but for a different reason. I hide behind my tiny peppermint bottle.

"Don't hesitate to call. Bobby Orville is going to be on the evening shift this week. I trained him myself. He's a good guy. See you soon."

He gets up; the couch re-levels itself and then feels empty. I hear the door click.

What's wrong with you, girl? I didn't even say goodbye. Not to mention . . . What?! Richard was murdered? What makes Mark think the murderer is still around and that I need a police detail? I curl up on the couch as all the questions I should've asked him flash across my mind. Is it safe to take Bugle out when nature calls? Am I supposed to tell Bobby if I'm going somewhere? Are they watching me or the building? If the first, why? Am I a suspect?

I get up and trade the peppermint for the lavender. I need to soak in hot, oily water. An hour later with my lavender-infused hair wrapped in a towel, my phone rings. Mark's face flashes on the screen. What on earth will he say this time?

"Hello?" Oh, look, I got a word out of my mouth.

"Hey, Stephanie. Would you . . . would you want to go out for dinner Saturday evening?"

My mouth drops open. Did he just ask me out? My voice actually responds, "Sounds good. What time?"

"How about six?" he questions.

"Perfect." I make a shocked face at Bugle.

"I'll pick you up then. How's that?"

"I'll be ready." I hang up and laugh out loud. Life is crazy.

FRIDAY, 5:50 A.M.

I leave for work early, packing a bottle of frankincense for Cindy. My mom's longtime friend is going in for some tests, and Mom had asked me to take her some. It had been the most unusual Thursday of my existence: got asked out by possibly the most handsome man I've ever seen, signed up my mom with Essential Sense, discovered a murderer might be lurking in my apartment building, and ordered three surveillance cameras from Amazon.

I pull up at Cindy's. A white van with no windows stops on the opposite side of the road. I bite my lip, hoping they will pull back into traffic. Nope. Gathering my courage, I open the car door.

"Stay," I say to Bugle; she watches out the window as I slip the bottle of oil through the old-style mail slot in Cindy's door. I hurry back to the car. Cindy's out for the day, but Mom will fill her in on how to use the oil.

A few minutes later, I pull my eyes off the rear-view mirror, where I'd been scanning for the white van. We pull into doggie daycare. Jerome braces for Bugle's leap into his arms.

"Well, Miss Stephanie, I have you down on the calendar to be leaving Bugle here full time from the twenty-sixth through the ninth. Is that correct?" Jerome asks.

"Yes, it is."

Jerome sits Bugle down and heads over to the computer. He knocks against the display of organic cotton collars, and I can't keep from straightening them.

"Okay, we are all set for that. We'll take the best care of Bugle baby."

"I know it. I still hate leaving her." Especially with everything that's happened lately.

"Any word on the case?"

I know he's asking about Richard. Jerome's young; I'm guessing maybe nineteen. He probably watches crime dramas all the time. "Well . . ." I have a hard time getting the words out. "The police have now labeled it a homicide."

Jerome's mouth makes a dramatic "O." "No kidding! Did they say what the murder weapon was?"

I pull back; I don't like the subject, and time is ticking. "I'm a little fuzzy on the details. See you, Buge."

THIEVES

I slide into my Herman Miller swivel chair and look at my desk. A cold feeling spreads up my arms. I am absolutely positive that I left the bottles of lavender and Relax tucked right under my computer monitor. They're still sitting there; the lavender bottle is just out of line with the Relax. I'd lined them up perfectly straight before I left work yesterday—just as I do with everything.

The unnerving change grips me. Homicide. Don't worry, the police will be watching over you. Why do you think I'm the one who needs protecting? Why are so many things in my apartment out of place? And now at work too. How far is shouting distance anyway?

Harry invades my doorway, and I beat him to words. "Were you in my office last night?"

He sneers in response. "I was at the officers' meeting, remember? The meeting you forgot to buy beverages for?"

Usually, this type of confrontation would've brought me into super stress. I don't forget Harry's lists. I just don't. That's what he pays me for. But today the out-of-place bottles so closely matching the ones in my bathroom have overtaken all other concerns. I make a guttural noise in response. "It was inexcusable. Sorry."

Surprisingly, my blunt response seems to deflect his wrath. "Get Jim Spoonburg on line one. Tell Melanie from HR to be in my office in ten minutes. Pull the files from the Rocky Point sale last August." He turns on his ten-thousand-dollar Louis Vuitton Manhattan heel, and I stand immediately.

I have to know about the oil bottles.

I walk toward the new blonde secretary, wishing I could remember her name.

"Good morning!" I say. "Could you look up the schedule for the office cleaners? Call me on my extension and let me know if they cleaned last night, will you?"

She looks up at me, her blue eyes showing relief that it's not Harry asking her for something. Poor girl. Fifteen minutes later my desk phone rings.

"Stephanie?" Her voice is cautious.

"Yes?" I respond.

"This is Ginny. I checked the cleaning schedule. They were here last Monday, and they're scheduled to come again on Monday of next week."

My stomach turns; I'd been hoping she would tell me someone had at least dusted the night before. "Thanks, Ginny." I file her name in my head as I hang up. My phone rings again while it's still in my hand.

"We've got a meeting tomorrow night. Get reservations at Salvador's, group of nine. Seven-thirty. Make sure my gray Brioni suit is clean and pressed. And where are the Rocky Point files?"

Really?! I've got a date tomorrow night. Harry hangs up. I hadn't said a word. I start clicking through sale files. A date with an intriguingly handsome guy or facilitate a meeting for my current tyrant?

I look back at my now perfectly aligned oils. There's a good chance someone is after me. Richard's face flashes up in my mind. I don't want to miss living. I don't want to regret anything. Suddenly, for the first time in my life, my job seems so petty and secondary to living life.

All this time and stress for what? What if it had been me on that staircase? Have I even lived yet? Ever loved someone? Ever given of myself to love someone? Someday I want a baby. This thought shocks me. I feel like I've been knocked loose from a place I've been anchored to for years. I watch a perfectly clear drop of lavender hang on the edge of the bottle before diving onto my wrist. I rub my wrists together and inhale. Maybe it's time for a change.

A few minutes later I slide Harry's precious files across his desk "Salvador's, the stateroom. Three extra servers. Your gray Brioni is clean, but it's in Utah. You'll have to wear the black one; it's here. I won't be at the meeting."

Harry hadn't bothered to look up when I walked in, but my last statement makes his head snap around with fire in his eyes. A waft of lavender hits me, and I square up to him. "Yes, you will." His dark eyes dare me to deny him.

"No, I won't. I have plans." Dishing out some of his own medicine, I whip around and exit his office, wondering if I have just lost my job.

CHAPTER FOUR

SATURDAY, 12:55 P.M.

"Beck, I need you. Bring your big curling iron and your toolkit." I hang up before she can answer. It makes me smile. I've got a lot to do before my date tonight.

Half an hour later, I open the door to find Beck standing there with her huge curling iron in one hand and a pink plastic toolbox in the other.

"What in the world?" she says.

Before she can say anything else, I smile and pull her through the door. "So. I'm pretty sure I'm being stalked."

Beck drops everything on the floor, her face white. "What? You're serious, aren't you? Did Mark tell you that?"

I pick up the iron. Whew, it doesn't look broken. I'm going to need it. "No. But he did say the police are watching me. Things have been out of place in my apartment and at work. Plus, there's this white van I keep seeing."

Beck's face goes a shade lighter. "I'd say the white van is definitely a bad sign." She swallows hard. "I saw one in the parking lot when I came in. Someone's been stealing your stuff?"

"No, it's like someone has been looking for something though. Things aren't like I left them," I say.

"You, my persnickety friend, would know too. This isn't funny, Steph. Aren't you scared?"

I pick up my bottle of Courage and pass it under my nose. "I'm okay—most of the time. Need to figure this out though. I was convincing myself that I was making it up, but I can't deny it any longer." I slide a mailing box over the counter between us.

"Plus, this came today." I wrestle a huge Essential Sense box across the floor. "It feels like Christmas! I can't wait to see what you ordered me." I rip open the box full of goodies and pull out a white-and-purple box with Superberry scrawled across it. I rip the top off a packet.

"Yum! It is so good!" I tip the packet way up. "I used to think the words 'healthy,' and 'yuck' were synonymous, but this is like, man, even better than berries!"

"It's true!" Beck agrees.

So, it's time to face reality. "We are going to put up a surveillance system," I state, as I open my Essential Mist diffuser and put six drops of Courage into the water.

"I can't believe we are doing something like this." Beck flips open the box and pulls out a tiny surveillance camera. "Look how small it is. How many did you get?"

"Three. I want one near the bathroom. Come on. Let's spy this place." I turn on some music, and we laugh at each other as we try to figure out how to hang the cameras out of sight.

Beck chips an acrylic nail when her screwdriver slips.

"Now I know you are a true friend," I say, picking up her tool.

"You can take me for a reset after we catch this guy."

I nod, handing her another Superberry packet.

"That will do the trick," she says, and I can't help drinking one with her. I walk out of the apartment, turn around and walk back in, waving at the wall.

From the bedroom, Beck's voice echoes, "Yep! Got you clear as can be. Okay, walk through the kitchen . . . now down the hall," she calls as she watches the livestream.

I walk through my house, pushing off a creeping fear. Will I ever feel safe again? I force myself to find peace. A verse from my childhood rises up from my heart: He will never leave you nor forsake you. Well, Lord, I need You now.

Soon I stand before Beck with my hands on my hips. "It's time," I say cryptically.

She stares at me, openmouthed.

Who knows what I might say next? I smile, enjoying having her on the edge because for once, I'm the one being unpredictable. "To get ready for my date."

Beck relaxes with a sigh. "Now that I can definitely help you with! Let me run out to the car; I've got all my Beauty Essence makeup this morning, plus what you got today."

Moments later I'm gazing at the entire line of Beauty Essence makeup. "How on earth did you get all this stuff? Did you buy it along with your starter kit?" I touch the tubs reverently.

"No, I put it on my first EB order. This is the best makeup I've ever worn. Absolutely weightless. Great coverage, lasting color, no chemicals." This is Beck's element; her makeup is always flawless.

"Well, I'm sold. How much money have you spent?"

Beck shakes her head as she sends me into the bathroom with three beautiful bottles labeled Fresh. "I'm not spending money, Steph. I'm investing in my business. Did you look at the compensation plan? Essential Sense is the best business opportunity I've ever come across. I'm doing it. That's that."

I emerge from the bathroom with my face feeling as if I've gone to a spa, trying to ignore the fact that I'm recording myself in my own home.

"Sit down and let me get your makeup done."

I close my eyes; the Beauty Essence brushes are so soft. It seems just a moment later that Beck snaps me out of my mental nothingness. She's holding a mirror in front of my face, and my mouth hangs open.

"I'm gorgeous. How did you do that?"

Beck laughs. "You're always gorgeous, I just did some contouring. That man doesn't stand a chance."

I snort in a very unladylike manner.

"Now for this," Beck whispers. She withdraws a pink-labeled bottle from her purse and hands it to me.

"Ylang ylang? Am I saying that right?" I question.

"Who cares? Open it and rub some into your hair; it's supposed to be quite the oil."

The sweet aroma of flowers envelops me. "Wow! That's incredible!" I look at the clock. "Fifteen minutes till he gets here!" I jet for my bedroom. "What am I gonna wear?"

Beck digs through my shoes and emerges with skimpy black heels. "Should I dress up that much?" Now I'm wishing I'd asked him where we were going.

Beck smiles a sinister grin. "The black dress you wore last Christmas."

I shake my head as I declare, "No way." That dress was a onetime deal.

"You don't have a choice; you're out of time." Beck holds it out. "The seconds are ticking. You can't go in your jeans."

I bite my lip then snatch the black, just-above-the-knee dress out of her hand. When I'm dressed, she hands me some deodorant.

"Oh, thanks." It smells so good I flip it over. Essential Sense Lavender Deodorant.

"How do you know so much about all these products? You've only had your kit a few days!"

"Me and Google are tight," she says, grinning as she curls the tips of my hair.

I look at the time; sweat breaks out as my stomach flutters.

Heading over to the window, I pull back the shade as a bright-blue Dodge Ram pulls in. Beck presses her face to the glass next to mine.

"That's him. Great truck. Off you go, girl." Bugle's snout smears the window.

"Oh! Bugle, you haven't been out in hours," I cry.

"Don't worry, Buge and I are good. I'll take care of her," Beck says.

I plop a kiss on Bugle's curls, and then I'm out the door with a little black purse in my hand.

A nervous smile plays on Mark's face as he walks around the back of the truck. He is so handsome in a black, long-sleeved button-down and khakis that seem to show off every muscle.

"Hi!" I kick myself for such a lame intro.

"You look great, Stephanie." He opens the truck door. How on earth am I going to climb up in there in this skirt? His big hand finds mine, sending a thrill up my arm as he helps me in. I've never been treated this way. I glance at the CB radio mounted under the dash but push all thoughts of crime dramas and the last week out of my mind. Tonight, he's just Mark.

"I thought we would go to Michael's down on the south side," he says as he seems to fill the truck with his presence.

"Sounds great; I've never been there." I buckle my seatbelt.

"It's Italian. The thing I like about the place is there aren't nineteen TVs playing everywhere."

I nod, smoothing my skirt.

SATURDAY, 7:58 P.M.

I find myself staring at Mark as he chats with the pretty waitress while paying the bill. Her name tag reads "Kaylee," and she's obviously been enamored with Mark from the second she laid eyes on him. I answer her in my mind.

"I'm so glad you came to Michael's tonight; it was such a pleasure to serve you."

Right, that's not an obvious offer, is it?

"Are you military or police force? You must be . . . to stay in such great shape."

Don't sound so desperate now, Kaylee. He might pick up on it.

"Wow! How long have you been a policeman?"

Why don't you just ask for his number and get it over with? I'll snatch it out of your hand the second he's not looking.

"Well, if you ever want a free meal, you just come on back. I work weekends, and I'll make sure you get all you want."

My face goes red. Hussy!

Mark seems oblivious though. His phone goes off with a persistent buzz. He snatches it up, looks at me after reading the text.

A blush creeps up my neck. Get it together, Stephanie!

"We gotta run. Would you mind coming with me on a call real quick?"

He stands up from the bench and extends his hand to help me. I slide mine into his. Wish it could stay there forever. Mark is in a hurry now, and I hustle to keep up. Glancing over my shoulder, I find Kaylee still staring. I smile, feeling as if I just won the lottery.

"So, that text was from my deputy. He doesn't call unless he seriously needs help. Could you sit in the truck for a few minutes?" he asks.

How could I resist? "Of course, whatever you need is fine."

Mark helps me in then jogs around the front. He flips on a blue light on the roof, looks over at me and grins. "Buckle up. We're in a hurry."

I can't help returning his smile as I snap my seatbelt closed. He floors it, his radio crackling, "Unit 220 involved in hand-to-hand, assistance requested." I shift to keep my balance as we race around corners and zip through red traffic lights.

"Could you get my vest from the backseat, Stephanie? Should be on your side." I twist around, reaching for the heavy Kevlar vest. I grunt as we whip left, and the seatbelt catches me. I pull till the vest comes free and haul it over the seat.

"Thanks. There should be a belt too. Can you reach it?"

"Yep." I twist again. The belt still has a thick baton attached to it. Blue lights are flashing ahead, sharp against the dim streetlights. Two officers are wrestling with a man in a front yard.

"Oh, no," Mark says. "He's on PCP. Sit tight, will you? Just lock the doors and don't get out." Mark swings out his door, slipping into the bulletproof vest as he starts to run.

I reach over, lock the doors, and watch in morbid fascination. Is he? Yep, the man the two policemen are fighting with is stark naked and glistening with sweat as fat jiggles everywhere. The officers are using the batons in an effort to subdue him, but the man seems impervious to their attempts and is bent on hurting somebody.

Mark reaches them, diving in. I hold my breath, hand outstretched on the dash. Mark's momentum knocks the naked man to the ground, and the officers pile up on him. Somehow, he slithers out of their grasp and is on his feet, kicking like a wildcat. Mark is up first and slams his bulk into the man again. Then everything is chaos as the other officers join in.

My nose is almost against the windshield. Something metallic flashes—a gun? I let out a breath; no, it's handcuffs. Even after his hands are behind his back, the man uses his head as a weapon. Mark leaps out of the way as the naked man tries to headbutt him.

Mark and the others are still busy holding down the first man when the front door suddenly opens, and another sweating man steps outside. At least he is still wearing underwear, but he's holding a gun.

"NO!" I shout. My breath fogs the windshield, and in the second it takes me to wipe it away, Mark has left the first man and is barreling toward the gunman with shocking speed. The gun bucks, there's a flash in the dim entryway, and Mark spins, hit hard in the chest. He takes the hit and keeps twisting till he's zeroed in on his target again. Before the gun can explode another time, Mark has flown the last three feet separating them. The two men disappear through the doorway.

My hands fly up to cover my mouth, willing him to reappear. "Oh, God Almighty, please keep him safe!"

More flashing blue lights race down the street. Four more officers race into the house. Seconds drag as I resist opening the door with everything I have.

Shadows move past the windows of the house, and finally three police officers exit. I practically melt when I see Mark among them. An ambulance flashes in the street and two paramedics converge on Mark. He reaches out with a handshake for the first one to greet him. I watch him deflect their efforts to examine him, from the firm handshake to outright backing away from the persistent EMT. He grins and waves, veering off toward me and unzipping his vest.

I slide back in my seat as he opens the door and jumps in. The vest lands with a thud on the armrest. My eyes find a frayed hole in the left chest panel. I look up to find his gaze on me. "I'm sorry you had to see that."

"Me too! How on earth did you get yourself to touch that guy? The sweat had to be awful." The stress gets to me, catching me off guard, and I flip into laughter. I can't help it; seeing the crazed naked man was just too much, and the giggles won't stop—no matter how hard I try.

Mark's brows lift, and amusement makes his eyes happy. "The key is not to think about it before you do it."

I snort and cover my mouth. "Why didn't he have any clothes on? Is that a normal night for you?"

Mark shrugs. "Sort of, I guess; they were on PCP. First, it makes them hot, then more than a little loopy, so they strip. As soon as you see a sweaty stripped person, your first guess should always be PCP. The drug also turns them into a freight train. If a guy I can usually take by myself is on that drug, it would take at least four guys to bring him down." Mark turns the ignition key.

"Let's get out of here before the EMTs change their minds. I had to bring to remembrance an old favor Tyler owes me in order to give them the slip. I feel bad enough to have dragged you out here. I don't want you to have to wait while they check me

59

out." He shifts in his seat.

"Are you all right though? Maybe we should stay." I finger the still hot hole in the vest. Mark puts the truck in gear and pulls out.

"Based on previous experience, I'd say I have about ten minutes until the adrenaline wears off, and I start to feel it." He smiles at me again, and I melt inside.

"Are you sure you shouldn't let them look at it? That's a pretty big hole in your vest."

Mark rubs his chest, "Yeah, it's just a bruise. Maybe a flesh wound." He pauses a second. "You want to get dessert somewhere?"

A smile curls one side of my mouth. He doesn't want it to end yet either. Still, we should get his chest cleaned up.

"How about a Frosty from Wendy's? You won't have to get out if we go through the drive-thru. Are you a chocolate or vanilla kind of guy?" I feel no remorse using Beck's inside info against him. We stop at a stop sign; he looks over at me, and the look in his eyes is hungry. His voice is low. "I'm vanilla all the way."

I nod, biting my lip. "Let's do it then."

We're in my parking lot, our Frosties almost gone. "I have some stuff that would help that bruise." About halfway through his ice cream, I noticed he'd quit holding it with his left hand and set it in the cup holder to finish, so I know he's hurting.

"It's nothing I'm going to have to arrest you for, is

it?" He jokes, and I hold up my hands in innocence.

"One hundred percent pure essential oils only." I pin him with my gaze. "Are you going to do anything other than take a shower and rinse it off?" He looks like a kid caught red-handed as he frowns.

"Nope." He scoops up the last of his dessert.

"All right then, come on."

Bugle dances wildly as we enter, and I kiss her on the head as I open my pocket reference for the essential oils app and type in "bruising." I gather up all the recommended oils that I have plus a carrier oil from the kitchen. Turning, I find Mark cuddling an extremely happy Bugle.

"Well, let's see what you've got." Mark straightens his left arm slowly. He uses only his right hand to unbutton his black shirt, and that's when I notice his right sleeve is ripped above the elbow.

"Did you hurt your arm too?" I ask.

Mark twists it, searching. "No, I think I just flexed too hard and ripped it."

I raise my eyebrows, puffing out my lips. I've never known a man who could rip his shirt by flexing. I watch him work at the buttons. He's never going to get the ones on his wrists off with one hand. I step in, hesitant.

He offers his right wrist smiling sheepishly. "My left arm's a little tight."

I unbutton his sleeves then reach up, finishing the two at his neck. Pulling off the black button-down reveals a tight white T-shirt complete with a bloodstain.

"Oh, you're bleeding!" Did we really go out for ice cream after he'd been shot?

"Uh-huh."

I look up from his chest to find him clearly unconcerned about the blood. "Well, we've got to get your other shirt off because that definitely needs to be cleaned."

"Sure." His voice is soft, but he doesn't move.

This close to him, I realize the top of my head only comes up to his shoulder. He seems completely content to stand there looking down at me. If he's not going to do it, I will. I lift his t-shirt, revealing six-pack abs. I bite my lip as I work the shirt up higher.

"You smell really nice." Mark's comment makes me look up at him; his eyes are intense.

"It's ylang ylang." Really, quite an oil. I have the shirt up to his armpits when I gasp. His entire left pec is bruised a deep blue shade, and a trickle of blood runs over his ribs. I touch his side, and he flinches.

"Sorry!"

He shakes his head. "It didn't hurt."

"Oh," I say, glancing up to find his eyes even more passionate. I drop mine. Focus, Stephanie! Focus on the job. "Okay, let's get your right arm first." I struggle with the tight fabric. He twists his arm, muscles bunching. This is fun. "There, now your head." I can't help admiring his neck and the muscles in his back. I swallow hard. "Let's just ease it off now." The shirt sticks around his bicep. My fingers brush his skin.

It's so soft. I step back, shirt in hand. I cannot believe such a gorgeous man is standing half-clothed in my living room. Oils! Come on, Stephanie, don't lose it now. "Let me get something to wipe up the blood." Soon I'm swabbing the point of impact with witch hazel and a drop of Germ Sniper oil.

"That looks better. I don't think the bullet is what made you bleed. I mean, of course it was, but I think the vest rubbed the skin too hard." I pour olive oil into my cupped palm and add three drops of Soothe and two drops of peppermint then mix it with my finger.

"Okay, I'll be as gentle as possible, but this might hurt a bit." I start at the center of the bruise and work the oil into it. His chest rises and falls faster. "Is that too much?"

"No," he whispers, so I keep going till I've used up all the oil, finally rubbing it in a wide circle on uninjured skin with my palms. This is the most enjoyable oiling I've ever done!

"You stayed in the truck." Mark's voice is husky. "Thank you for staying in the truck. When I saw that gun come out, all I could think of was a stray shot hitting you."

My stomach grows warm. He was thinking about me while getting shot, while overpowering crazy naked people on drugs. A whisper is all that will come out. "I'm a good listener."

Mark's head drops just a bit. "I like that."

I hesitate. For me, this is uncharted territory.

Mark's right hand reaches out to rub a drop of

oil that's collected on his ribs. He runs the same hand across his stubbled chin, his fingers brushing the corner of his mouth.

"Oh! You shouldn't have done that!" I say, eyes wide.

"Done what?" he questions.

"It's a hot oil! Your lips are going to feel like they're on fire in a second." I step closer, thinking to wipe it off, but his huge right arm circles my waist and draws me tight against him.

"Yes, they will," he whispers right before he kisses me.

I tug him closer and time stops.

He pulls back just a bit, and his eyes widen. "You weren't kidding! They do burn!"

"Told you," I whisper as my own lips start to tingle.

His hand is warm against the small of my back as he draws me close again. "I suppose I should share?" he asks, and I pull his head down again, memorizing everything about the moment.

When he finally lifts his head, he looks at me with a sly grin. "So, the next time I get shot, will you doctor me up again?"

I pull my lips to one side, considering. "How about you don't get shot, and I'll just doctor you for fun?" My face gets warm.

He grunts, grin growing. "That sounds like a deal."

I smile. Did I just make that offer?

Mark sighs. "I'd better go; you're too intoxicating for me to stay much longer. Could you throw this one out?" He hands me his t-shirt.

"Sure." I take it as I help him back into the button-down.

"Bobby's on duty tonight." He looks down at his unbuttoned shirt. "Could you button it back up? The last thing I need is some crazy rumor running through the station."

"Wouldn't be that bad, would it?" As I glance up at him coyly, a slow smile spreads across his face.

"No, no it wouldn't." He pauses for a moment then adds, "Do you want to come to church with my mom and me tomorrow?"

"That sounds great." Any time with you I can get, I'll take it!

CHAPTER FIVE

Beck sits next to me on the couch and hands me a bowl of popcorn. I sigh. The weekend had been perfect from start to finish. Except for Mark getting shot, but then again if that hadn't happened . . . She pushes play on the remote, and there I am in black and white on the screen walking down the hall and waving.

"Mmm, this popcorn is so good," I say. Bugle is cuddled up next to me, and I slip a buttery piece in front of her nose. Her tail beats a happy rhythm as she crunches it.

"That makeup is sweet, isn't it?" Beck says as we watch her apply it on me for my date. She doesn't wait for me to answer. "I signed up three more people with Essential Sense today. You'd better get in gear; I'm going to outrank you soon." She stuffs in another handful of popcorn.

I look over at her. "I've been busy lately." The me of two days ago looks at the time and disappears into the bedroom, emerging in the black dress.

"Sheena called; she wants us to go to business training in Dallas next weekend," Beck mumbles around her mouthful.

"Can't," I say, "I'll be in Utah."

She grunts in response. "This is like watching an old mime video. It's so weird not to hear us talking," Beck says, then makes a tsking sound. "Look how skinny you are! How do you do it? We binge the same junk food, but you stay so thin!"

I stuff another huge mouthful of popcorn in and answer around it, "Fasht matablizzmmm."

We watch me exit the apartment. Beck gets Bugle's leash, and they disappear out the door. She fast forwards till they come back in. The black and white Beck gets Bugle a treat; then they play tug till Bugle goes for a drink. Beck kisses her on the head and then leaves, locking the door.

"Aw! You are the best," I tell her.

"I know," Beck responds.

We watch Bugle run from window to window then start to chase her tail. Now I know what she does when I leave. Beck hits fast forward after Bugle lies down. Soon enough she's up again, wagging her tail at the door.

"Oh no," I say, thinking about what had transpired after Mark brought me home.

"What?" she asks, immediately interested.

"Give me the remote." I hold out my hand, and Beck's eyes narrow as she takes in the blush that is creeping up my neck.

"No way!"

I snatch at it, but she's too fast. She looks back at the screen; her mouth swings open as Mark and I come in.

"He came up?! You so left that part out."

I lunge for the remote again then deeply consider wrestling her for it. She'd probably beat me anyway. Besides, nothing X-rated happened, and so, yeah, I could watch it again.

By the time I'm smearing oil on the bruised side of Mark's chest, Beck is throwing a fit. "How could you? Ahhh! He is so handsome. Who is this woman on the screen? Surely it is not my celibate, OCD best friend!" She sucks in her breath when he draws me closer. "Whhaattt?" she cries, and I grunt in satisfaction. It's all in the open now.

"Oh, yeah," I say with a smirk. "It was better than it looks on the grainy recording too." When she looks at me, shocked, I say, "It was the ylang ylang."

Beck nods, perfectly convinced. "What's he saying? I have to know," Beck pleads.

My fingers play over my lips remembering. "Never gonna happen, Beck. Those words are all mine. And I remember every single one." I grin at her, rubbing it in.

I watch as the Mark in black and white hands me a stained shirt and heads out the door.

My smile turns sheepish as I withdraw the very same shirt from the storage bin that's built into my coffee table.

"No!" she says, incredulous.

"Yes. I kept it." I hold it up as she comes over to gawk at the bloodstain. "It really happened, Beck. I saw it, but I just can't believe it."

She touches the shirt reverently.

I hug the shirt, burying my nose in it.

She cries, "Oh man! Oh man, it's happened! You are in love." She engulfs me in a hug.

I shake my head, but I can't quite deny it.

Stashing the shirt again, I pick up my popcorn and start munching. Beck goes on reveling, and I can't believe I didn't think of that being on camera. We fast-forward the night, and then there I am dancing in the kitchen, starting coffee, and texting Beck to tell her I won't be at church with her as usual.

Soon Bugle is running from window to window again, chasing her tail after I leave, and then finally curling up on her bed. Beck clicks fast-forward but scowls as Bugle is back up seconds later. Barking and wagging at the door.

"Did you forget something and come back up?" Beck questions.

"Um," I think hard. "No, I didn't."

Beck rewinds, counts off exactly three minutes from the time I shut the door to go to church till Bugle is up at the door again.

"Must be someone walking down the hall." I backpedal mentally. "Maybe I don't want to see this."

Beck scoots closer to me, whispering, "We need to watch it." Her hand finds my knee with a death grip as the door eases open.

"You're sure you didn't come back up?"

Tears well up in my eyes as a hooded figure slips through my door. Bugle is barking wildly, jumping hard at the man.

I grab my pup and hold her close. "Baby, you were trying to protect our house," I say as we watch the tall man walk to the counter. His gloved right hand goes right into the treat bin.

I gasp. "He knows where I keep the treats. He knows when I leave for church. He knows everything!"

In the video, Bugle runs to her bed to munch her treat. I whisper, "Traitor." Beck's hand finds mine, and we sit clutched with terror as we watch the man pilfer my apartment. He disappears into my bathroom.

I try not to hyperventilate. "Stuff's always been different than I left it in there." I squeeze Beck's hand harder, and tears fall as I consider the implications.

"Ouch," Beck whispers as I force myself to let go.

"How long has he been breaking into my apartment? Why me? Does he break into every apartment in the building? Or just mine? But, no, things have been out of place at work too, so it must be just me."

My eyes widen. "I can't do this. I can't . . ." I gasp for air. "Did Richard catch him in the act? Oh! Is this who killed Richard? Is a murderer giving treats to my dog?"

Beck shakes me. "Call Mark right now. Is he on duty? Call him up; he has to see this."

I nod, tapping his icon with my finger and so glad to see his handsome face pop up on my screen. "Mark?" My voice is pinched and funny. "Are you working?"

His deep voice settles me a little. "Yeah, I'm on duty. Are you okay?"

"No. I'm not. Can you come over and look at something?"

He's quiet for a second. "After work or now?" I hear his real question: are you wanting the man or the officer?

"Now." My voice is still too high.

"Bobby's on duty at your place; you want him to come in?" I swallow hard. At least there's someone trustworthy nearby.

"No, I just want you." I think about changing that statement, but it's the truth so I don't.

"Give me twenty minutes. I'm turning around now."

I let out a breath. "Thanks," I say and hang up.

Beck interrupts, "Listen, Steph, you can't sleep here tonight. Go pack up for you and Bugle to sleep at my place tonight. While you're doing that, I'm going to cut this recording so that your hot little doctor session doesn't end up being attached to it."

I look at her then fall on her neck and hug her. "What would I do without you? Thanks, Beck. You're the best."

She smiles. "I've heard that before."

It seems as if only seconds pass until Bugle is at the door barking. I open it in a cloud of Relax. Mark stands there like a wall. I smile with half my mouth, instantly safe in his presence. "Thanks for coming. How is your chest?"

He shrugs both shoulders, showing off the movement. "It's really good actually. I've been putting on that oil you gave me Sunday. What's up?"

I back up, drawing him into my home. Beck is theatrically dragging my bags down the hallway.

"Oh, this is my best friend, Rebecca Graham. We've been friends since. . ." I pause, trying to think when we met.

Mark finishes for me, "Since your freshman year at Shaw University." He extends a strong hand toward Beck. One of her black eyebrows arches up as she shakes it.

"I researched you pretty well when you found the body, Stephanie; it's standard procedure."

I shake my head. These are two peas in a pod on the background thing. "So." Where to start? "I'm sort of OCD with my stuff." Beck and Mark both stare at me blankly. Okay, so maybe that was obvious. "But I keep finding things out of place. I always leave my toothbrush with the bristles up, straight along the sink."

Mark breaks in, "Duly noted."

I roll my eyes. "Anyway, sometimes when I get home it's flipped on its side. I know, I know, but it's been a lot of things. Even at the office. So, I bought a surveillance system. I had to know what was going on. Beck and I installed it this weekend."

Mark's eyes get a little wider. Clearly, our oily kiss is still fresh on his mind. "This weekend?" he questions.

Beck answers before I can. "Don't worry, I cut that part out."

His eyes widen and swerve over to Beck who's smiling wickedly. I smack my forehead with my hand and pin her with my eyes. She stares back at me brazenly. "Because I know you and how much you like it!" she adds.

Mark's eyebrows go up, and a slow smile spreads over his face as he looks at me.

I hold out both my hands. "Okay, people. The point is, I have footage of someone breaking into my apartment."

Mark straightens. "What?"

"Yeah," is all I say because I don't want to start crying in front of him.

"Come on." Beck powers on my TV and starts the Sunday morning clip with me walking out the door for church. I count the three minutes off in my head. He watched me get into my car, then he came in. He watched me.

Mark's arms cross his chest, but he leans forward when the door eases open. I watch in horror as my fur baby jumps hard at the evil intruder. The video runs out with his exit.

Mark snatches the remote successfully from Beck and replays the clip. He's all business now, getting the details.

"You're right. This isn't his first time in. Can I—?"

Beck cuts him off by slapping a flash drive of the video into his palm.

"Thanks." He's quiet for a moment, thinking.

Beck breaks the silence, "She's coming home with me. Both her and Bugle."

Mark scratches his stubbly chin. "All right. I'm sure she would be fine here though. I'll get this video over to the petty theft guys."

Beck's nose wrinkles up in disgust. "But he didn't steal anything. He left empty-handed."

"True. Still, I have to get this into the right hands." He looks at me. "So you're going?"

I nod, more than a little shocked at his seeming dismissal of the situation. "Yeah." My voice comes out flat.

"All right, I'll be in touch." He disappears out the door.

Beck turns around with a hurt look on her face. "Well, he didn't give that much credit, did he?" she says.

I burst into tears.

"Oh, Steph! I shouldn't have said that. Come on, let's get Bugle's leash, and we'll go, okay?" She rubs my back until I get it together.

"All this stress makes me want to cook. I'm going to make something good," Beck says.

Tuesday afternoon crawls along, and I feel as if I've been hit by a bus. I hadn't slept, wrestling with the images of the two men in my apartment—one I wish had never been there, and the other I desperately wish would remain. But his casual treatment had hurt me deeply. How could he be so unconcerned?

I clench my teeth as Harry berates me again for not being at the Saturday meeting. I'd wondered what he would do about my refusing to go with them. Now I know.

"Don't you dare forget to finish that email to Horton equipment and copy me on it."

Oh, that's a low blow after all these years, Harry. Now I have to send you my communications? I stare him down. Why do I put up with him? Crossing my arms, I look over his shoulder at the clock. Ten more minutes.

Harry catches my slight and turns to see what I'm looking at. He points his finger at me. "You're on thin ice, Stephanie Pierce." Then he's gone.

I type the email, copy him, and leave five minutes early. As I step out the front door of the building, a white van pulls into the lot. I freeze, my hand still on the door. You've seen too many movies. I can't get a good view of the driver. The windshield catches the sun, and all I can make out is a tall thin figure. He sits, waiting. For me? I bite my lip then slide back into the building. Peering around the door frame, I watch as the van lurks in the lot. If it was a delivery van, surely the driver would be delivering something. A sour taste rises in my mouth as the minutes tick by. Finally, the van pulls out. I grip my keys and run to my car.

It's cold and gray outside—unusual for North Carolina, but it fits the day. The ten-minute drive to get Bugle from doggie daycare stretches into thirty-five because the traffic is so bad. I'm scanning for white vans behind me the entire time. Adrenalin flares through my chest twice when I catch sight of it, far back in traffic. Finally, I'm on my knees snuggling Bugle after Jerome brings her out.

"Hey, baby," I whisper as I kiss her head. The tension drains away as I pet her.

"Rough day?" Jerome asks. He's a likable person—even more than the girl who had worked here a few months ago.

"You wouldn't believe it. Sometimes I wish I had your job, Jerome. No stress." I smile sadly.

He laughs. "But then you would have to drive a car like mine." He points to his dented white Camry parked in the lot. "And we wouldn't see you or Bugle anymore."

I frown. It's true. If I didn't work for Harry, I wouldn't have to leave Bugle all the time. "We all have to start somewhere," I say, and he nods.

"That's right. Hey, we've got some new pup shampoo in. Why don't you take a look at it?"

I smile for the first time today. Shopping for Bugle always makes me happy.

"We've got two new scents: Honey Oat and Sweet Jasmine." Jerome's long fingers unscrew the Sweet Jasmine lid and pass it under my nose. If I hadn't smelled the ylang ylang, I probably would have liked it, but it just smells fake compared to the oil.

"Uhh," I say, so he unscrews the Honey Oat lid. I sniff it; it's not too bad. I take it, juggling Bugle's leash as I look for the ingredients list.

"Whoa," I say. "That's a lot of chemicals." Doesn't Essential Sense have pet shampoo? Just then as Jerome is leaning in to look at the list, the door opens, and Bugle hits the end of the leash as she rushes to greet a black lab coming in.

"Oh!" I say as the leash snaps taut. It had wrapped around the bottle, and it seems like an eternity passes as I watch the thick slop of shampoo vomit out of the bottle and fly directly into Jerome's unsuspecting face. He reels back when it hits him, wiping wildly at his eyes.

"I'm sorry! I'm so sorry!" I rush, tugging Bugle to grab a stack of wipes they keep handy for puppy accidents. "Here! Here, Jerome." I stuff the wipes into his slimy hands.

"Ouch! Oh, that stings." He's gotten the worst of it off his skin, but his eyes were open when it spewed onto him. He rolls his eyes hard, seeking relief, and I catch a glisten of emerald green. I grab more wipes, but then change my mind. Instead, I usher him through the double doors and back into the wash bay. Leann, the owner looks up.

"What on earth?" Her face is horrified.

"Bugle and I shot him with shampoo! I'm so sorry."

Leann takes over, forcing Jerome to bend over the dog wash bay.

"Hold your breath," she commands right before she shoots him in the face with warm water. The poor kid sputters and spits while the shampoo foams up.

"Ah! Stop!" he cries, standing straight and rolling his red eyes again.

This time I catch another flash of green. I realize he's wearing colored contacts. Why would anybody with such incredibly gorgeous green eyes want to cover them up with dull brown contacts?

Leann grabs the back of his neck again. "Nope, you've got to flush them for at least ten minutes, Jerome." Under he goes again. Finally, Leann allows him to plunk down in a chair with a towel over his eyes.

I stand there watching, feeling two inches tall.

Jerome says. "Miss Leann, I don't think that new shampoo is safe for dogs. What if you got it in their eyes?"

"Jerome, you're one-of-a-kind . . . and you're absolutely right." Leann's short blond hair catches the light as she shakes her head.

Leann looks over at me. "No harm done. Go on home, Stephanie. He'll be all right." I back through the doors with Bugle as I repeat, "I'm so sorry, Jerome."

CHAPTER SIX

I stare blankly at my computer Wednesday morning. I didn't sleep last night. Again. Beck had asked me to stay with her, but what am I going to do? Just move in with her? Wouldn't the creep just figure it out? So, I'd crushed up a bag of chips and poured them on the floor in front of my door. Then I'd dragged Bugle away from munching them and slept in my bedroom, listening for footsteps crunching on potato chips. Well, she had slept, and I had laid awake.

I'd also ignored all of Mark's calls, and there were a lot of them. Finally, a blonde officer with Orville on his name tag had knocked on the door. I had answered, pajamas and all. He informed me that Officer Wellborn had asked him to check on me. "Are you all right?"

I almost lost it. Sure! I'm all right. I'm tough. I can handle bodies, stalkers, nasty bosses, and men who don't care. Just watch me. I got essential oils, baby! But I kept my cool, and I told him I was good. Bobby had stood there staring at the potato chip mess between us, putting two and two together. "I'll be around all night," he informed me. I think I left quite an impression.

My cursor blinks at me. I have no clue what I'm supposed to make it do. Jerome's poor face flashes up into my mind. His eyes were still swollen and red this morning.

I look up to find Harry at the door with a stack of files in his arms. Without a word, he drops them onto my desk from a foot in the air. They splatter down in disarray. He knows it will drive me crazy. Then he turns on his heel and walks out. I stare at the files; I totally don't care that they are askew.

Jerome's words come back to me. Bugle wouldn't have to be there anymore. I think about my plane ticket to Utah for tomorrow. I don't want to go. I don't want to leave Bugle again. I don't want to spend two weeks with Harry. I don't ever want to see Harry again.

I turn back to my computer screen and open my online banking. I click on my savings account and stare at the impressive number. I've been building it so carefully for years. Maybe it has become too important to me. I've been sacrificing more important things for it.

I look down at my lavender bottle. Then I click to the Essential Sense website and pull up the compensation plan. I study the numbers carefully for a long time. Ruby. I would need to become a seller at the level the company calls "Ruby" in order to equal my current salary. What's stopping me? I sit up straight in my chair. Nothing. Nothing is stopping me. I can read. That's all Sheena had done; she'd read to a group of people from a script. I can do that.

I click back to my savings account. I can live off of it while I build my Essential Sense business. I can—especially after I cancel my lease in Utah. Logging out I feel light, almost weightless, like I'm free. I straighten the files, not because I have to, but because I can. Picking up my trash can I take it out to the restroom and throw away the bag. All my personal things should fit in the basket. I'm surprised that my belongings fill less than half of it. I nestle the nearly empty Relax, then the lavender on top. It's time.

I go down to Harry's door. It's shut; that means he's on the phone. I open the door, breaking the golden rule, and Harry scowls at me. I walk up, press the disconnect button on his desk phone. His face turns red as a beet. I have always wanted to do that.

"I quit." I wait for his reaction. Who knows what he'll throw at me?

"You can't quit because you're fired!" Harry shouts.

I throw my head back and laugh. "No way, Harry. I beat you to it fair and square. I already quit."

His jaw clenches as I turn and exit. "Get back in here!" he thunders.

For the first time, I ignore Harry Thorn.

THIEVES

I pull up at the doggie daycare, my basket seat-belted next to me. I float through the door. Jerome peers at me through red eyes. Sure seems as if I smell essential oil. Can't quite put my finger on it though. Maybe Jerome put some sort of ointment on his poor red eyes.

He squints at me. "Is that you, Miss Stephanie?" He peers at the clock next. "You're kind of early, aren't you?"

My phone goes off; I bite my lip. It's Mark again, and I just can't deal with him right now. I click "ignore."

"Yes, I am. I want Bugle. I quit my job, so she won't have to stay here anymore," I say, my voice giddy.

"What?" Jerome says, "You quit your good job? Why?"

"Money isn't everything, Jerome. Besides, I found a better opportunity."

He stands there staring at me as if I'm crazy.

"I want Bugle," I state again.

He shakes his head in disbelief. "All right, Miss Stephanie." He goes to the kennel door, misses the handle, and tries again. Soon Bugle is licking me as I hug her.

"So, should I cancel the dates for your trip to Utah?" Jerome questions.

I nod. "Oh yes, take Bugle off your list. Entirely.

I'm going to take care of her now. Come on, girl, let's go. Goodbye, Jerome." I wave as we walk out the door. I'm feeling better by the moment.

"What do you say, girl? Should we get a burger to celebrate?"

She grins at me in the rearview mirror, tongue hanging out the side of her mouth.

"Let's do it. Max Burgers, here we come!" It's the best spot for a real homestyle burger, but it's sort of out in the country. In a few minutes, the traffic thins and then the buildings till we're driving past trees. I'm in no rush. None at all. All I have to do right now is buy burgers.

Flashing blue lights ruin my plan. I pull to the side, willing the patrol car to keep going. Nope. I sigh in disgust, putting the car in park. I lean forward, forehead against the steering wheel. There's a crisp knock on the window, and Bugle barks from the backseat. I sigh and lift my head. Mark Wellborn fills my view. I stare at him through the window as he pulls off his aviator sunglasses. Why does he have to be so devastatingly handsome?

Briefly, I imagine flooring it, just not dealing with this blip of my life. But then I remember the surveillance video. All of it. It's not something I can ignore. Not the first half, not the second half.

I roll down the window, and Bugle goes wild, wiggling and sticking her head through the tiny crack between my seat and the car. Mark reaches in to rub her curly head.

"Hey," he says, giving me a chance to respond.

I fail.

"Been trying to get you."

I nod. Still staring at him. He's so irresistible. I muster the hurt I'd felt like a wall, but it crumbles.

"Left work early?" His massive elbows rest on my door panel, his face only inches away. I shiver. Bugle's anteater-length tongue reaches out, catching his chin.

"Quit," I say.

Mark responds, "She's all right."

"No. I mean, I quit my job."

One dark brow goes up. "Really?" He absorbs the information. "Come on. We're going for a drive," he says, but when I don't move, he reaches in and hits the unlock button, then stretches over me for Bugle's leash. He also snatches my keys out of the ignition. Bugle leaps out, and I watch in the rearview mirror as Mark opens the back door of the patrol car, and she jumps in. Traitor. A second later he's back.

"Stephanie, if I have to carry you to the car, I will."

I frown up at him, replaying his speed as he tackled the naked guy. Probably couldn't outrun him—especially in my open-toed shoes.

I roll up my window before I open the door, since he took my keys, and it won't go up if I open the door first. Still, I sit for a second with it up, just to get under his skin. I succeed.

Grabbing my purse, I twist out of the car, catching my nylons on the seat. "Tsk," I say as a run appears down my calf. I stand up, but Mark doesn't back off. I look way up at his face. He smells so good.

"Thank you," he says.

Heat spreads up from my stomach. Not trusting my voice, I turn away and plop into the passenger seat of his patrol car. I've never sat in a police cruiser before. It's like a spaceship: laptops, radios, switches. Extra gun clipped to the side of the armrest.

The car rocks as Mark folds himself into the driver seat. He pushes the lock button on my key fob, and my taillights flash obediently. He pulls out, and the blue lights shut off. Two radios crackle at once. He reaches up and turns them down.

He weaves through the light traffic; brake lights flash everywhere as people slow down when they catch sight of us. Weird. His blinker ticks as we near the Kiwanis Park sign. I read it as we pass: twenty-four acres, dog run, playground, walking paths. He parks and then flicks the radio on his chest.

"I'm on lunch," he says before he unzips his vest and shrugs out of it. Then he clips on Bugle's leash and there they are—my two favorite beings on the planet waiting for me. I sigh as I slide out, and Mark and Bugle stride off toward the wooded path. I rub on some Courage, then follow, gathering myself. Strength rises from somewhere deep inside. Bugle stops at nature's call, and I catch up.

Mark turns, watching me. "You're angry with me," he states, clearly hoping to open some kind of communication between us.

I've been rude long enough. "I'm . . ." What do I

say? I desperately needed you to comfort me, but you just left? "I'm not sure I can trust my emotions right now. I may have overreacted."

He nods as we set off again. "I had a string of revelations as I watched your video that set me on edge. One of those was that the perpetrator seemed really comfortable. It wasn't his first time inside your apartment."

"Yeah, I thought that too. Do you think Richard caught him breaking in, and that's why he was killed?" I feel as if a light breeze would knock me over.

Mark looks down at me, his eyes gentle. "I hoped you hadn't thought of that. It could be. But the tape gave me what I needed to switch you from a witness to a potential victim. Time was of the essence though, and in order to keep an eye on you one hundred percent of the time, I had to get back to the station and file a protection order."

"That's why you knew where I was to pull me over?" I question.

"Yeah, an unmarked has been with you since Monday night. Listen, I thought I recognized the guy on your tape from somewhere."

"How?" I ask. "You can't see his face in the video."

"No, but I've been a policeman for years. You learn to watch people. He's familiar to me somehow, the way he moves, his build. I know I've seen him before. It's been driving me crazy. I've been going through all the wanted lists trying to find him."

Bugle stops to sniff, and Mark turns toward me.

"I'm sorry I left like I did. I'm sorry I didn't explain what I needed to do. I knew you needed me, but I had to get an official protection order for you. Technically, we shouldn't even be here. I shouldn't have close contact with a witness like this. I should have done it all differently. It's just I've never been . . . well, it's never been you before."

I look up, searching his face. "Oh," is all that will come out of my mouth, as usual. But inside everything has now changed.

He plunges on, "I . . . I was engaged once. Leah was killed by a drunk driver two weeks before the wedding. I told myself I wasn't going to do that again. I'd just stay single. But there you were with your shoe stuck in the staircase. Perfect. I haven't been able to get you off my mind since then." He lets out a deep breath, and I realize he's risking it all—his heart, possibly his job.

"When you showed me the video, it clicked that probably Richard was a casualty of the guy's normal habit of breaking into your apartment. It really got to me. I didn't want you to see how much it bothered me, and I probably went too far the other way." He pauses, looking as vulnerable as a six-foot-two-inch stacked dude can look. "So, I've done all the talking. Are we good? Or am I going have to pull you over every time I want to talk to you?"

The difference between Mark and Harry is so clear. Light to dark. Blessing to cursing. I just tossed Harry out of my life; maybe it really is time for something new. I open my mouth, and something incredible happens. I start to say exactly what I want to in Mark's presence. "You caught me off-guard. Off-balance."

Then words fail me again as something inside me hangs back. How can I trust anything going on in this chaos right now? How can I know if what I feel for Mark is just a part of my desperation for safety or if it's real? I shake my head. Trying again. "I'm sorry. Things are spinning so far out of my control, and I froze up. To answer your question, we're good, and thanks for watching out for me. I guess your job would be easier if I picked up the phone."

"Much," he says as Bugle tugs us down the path. "Are you staying at Beck's tonight?"

I shake my head. "No, I wasn't going to. I mean, should I just run away? If he's really after me, won't he just find me? And then she'd be in trouble too."

Mark turns back to me, extends his hand. Inside I hesitate, with too much swirling in my heart. But looking at him, how can I refuse? I watch my hand stretch out until it disappears inside his. He pulls me close, right up to his chest, as his arms envelop me. And he holds me. Just holds me. My cheek is against his chest, the steady rhythm of his heart in my ear. I relax and let my eyes slide shut, and for just a moment, nothing is in my mind except knowing that right now I'm safe.

I don't know how long he stands there like that,

just giving me what I need. But eventually, a happy thought rises, and I tilt my face up, smiling at Mark.

"Since I quit my job, I'm free. No more Harry."

One dark brow goes up in amusement. "I bet you gave him what for, didn't you?" he asks.

I laugh. "I'll probably think of exactly what I should've said to him in about two hours. But when I did come into his office to quit, he was talking on the phone. He ignored me, so I pressed the off button."

Mark smiles as his fingers trace my face.

I inhale. Oh, he smells so good. "What are you wearing anyway? I know it's an oil." He is positively intoxicating.

He grins wide. "Your best buddy slipped me a little something called Man Up Oil."

I shake my head in mock disgust. "She's always meddling."

"I'll take all the help I can get, Miss 'You'll Have to Pull Me Over.' You want to get a burger? We're only about a mile from Max's."

I almost missed what he said, staring at the pulse in his neck and thinking about kissing it. I nod in response, gathering myself. "That's where Buge and I were headed."

"Good, I'm hungry." I feel a little empty as he releases me and just a bit shocked that he hadn't kissed me. He must catch the thought glimmering in my eye because in a second, I'm back in his arms.

"You listen here, Stephanie Pierce, I'm not out to

take advantage of you. I plan on having all the time I like to kiss you." His voice lowers, and my stomach does a flip. "And that will be a lot." His head lowers just a bit, "But right now, what you needed was a hug—just to be loved. You can't tell me I'm wrong." He pauses waiting for me to deny it.

I don't.

"Just don't forget my plan, Stephanie Pierce. It gets better all the time."

WEDNESDAY, 1:00 P.M.

I take a huge bite of possibly the best burger I've ever tasted. Watching Mark eat is fun. He loves food. I swallow, shifting on the hard metal picnic bench.

"So, is being a law enforcement officer what you've always wanted to do?"

He shakes his head as he chews. "Nope. I just wanted to make a difference." He shrugs.

I could sit and stare at him all day.

"But after a few years I realized I'm not doing that where I am. I'm just holding back the tide. You know what I really want to do?"

"What?" I asked, enraptured.

"I want to coach football. High school. Those kids need somebody to show them what it means to be a man, how to treat people, how to win and lose and keep trying. That's where I can make an impact. Before they get to the age where I have to deal with them now."

I melt inside. Essential Sense, I'm going to

grow you until he can do everything in his heart without worrying about money. My eyes widen. I'm already thinking like we're married. Heat races up my throat and into my face.

"You sure are cute when you blush."

I look over at Bugle licking her bun-less burger tray.

"By the way, my mom is in love with you. She wants to buy one of those oil kit things."

My eyes swerve back to Mark, and a slow smile spreads over my face. My purse vibrates, and I dig for my phone. The blood drains right back out of my face when I see the notification.

"What?" Mark's last few fries stop halfway to his mouth.

I will the alert from my security system to disappear. "Beck linked the cameras to my phone. It's supposed to send me a notification if there's any activity at my house when my phone isn't present." My hand shakes. "It's notifying me . . ."

Mark clears the table with a leap, his shadow behind me making the phone even brighter. He reaches over my shoulder and clicks the notice. The phone blinks black, and then there's my living room with a hooded man striding down the hall. My blood runs cold. Suddenly, Mark's gone. I twist on the bench, watching him snatch his vest out of his car, radio to his mouth.

"Bugle! Come on!" I pull her away from her empty tray. "Get in!" I order, and she hops into the back seat.

"Bobby, get into three twelve-stat. Live B&E, my

ETA four minutes, BOLO for assault. Requesting additional backup, Circle Court Apartments."

Mark and I hit the seats, and we take off, lights flashing. I grip the armrest, fingers white, eyes glued to the phone. The hooded figure is reaching for the doorknob to exit, but he hesitates and leaps back and ducks behind the counter. My door eases open, and a pistol peeks through the opening, followed by the officer named Bobby Orville who checked on me the other night.

He sweeps my apartment with his gun, crouched and ready. I want to shout, He's in the kitchen! As Bobby starts down the hall, the top of the hood appears over my counter. My stalker explodes feet-first over the barrier flipping backward and landing cat-like behind Bobby. The gun goes off, and the flash of light is eerily silent in the security video. The hooded man spins and closes in. Bobby's gun flies out of his hands and smacks against my tile backsplash as the man's foot slams hard into Bobby's grip.

Bobby swings his fist, but his opponent's movement is so fast as he twists forward that he catches Bobby hard in the chin. In the next instant, his arm snakes around Bobby's neck. I catch a flash of something in his hand before it plunges toward Bobby's neck. Bobby fights, but his movements aren't strong. He staggers, then drops like a rock as the hooded man races for the door.

Someone is shouting.

"He's down! Bobby's down! He injected him with

something!" Mark growls, and I realize it was me shouting.

Mark flicks his radio, "EMTs immediate response, apartment three twelve, officer down." I speak over Mark so he can keep reporting.

"In the neck! Left side!"

"Chemical injection to the left side of the neck. What's your ETA?"

The radios blare, and I can't keep all the voices straight. We whip into my parking lot, my finger trembling as I point ahead to a man in a hood walking away. Mark's foot almost goes through the floor, the engine roars, and the man begins to run. He veers toward an embankment that drops five feet to the parking lot next door. He disappears around a shop as Mark cranks the wheel, and we slide toward the embankment. He slams into "park" as he catapults out of the patrol car and down the embankment into the lot. Mark's arms are pumping as he runs in search.

Blue lights snap me out of my stupor. I vault over the seat, shut Mark's door and hit the lock button. Bugle barks at Mark as he turns into an alleyway and disappears. I look over an find My neighbor, Sam, watching me from under the alcove. I turn, searching for Mark, and when I swivel back around, he's gone.

A sharp rap on my window makes me jump. A female officer points down at the lock button. It's hard to hit it I'm shaking so bad.

"Ma'am, where's Officer Wellborn?"

I point toward the shopping center. "That way."

Her thumb flicks the radio on her chest. "On foot pursuit headed north past Jones' Department Store. Assistance needed."

I find my voice. "Is Bobby all right?"

The woman's blue eyes soften. "They should be bringing him down any minute, ma'am." My entire parking lot is packed with police cars and ambulances. I cover my mouth as the stretcher exits my building; four EMTs run toward the ambulance. Its siren wails as it heads to the hospital.

It's all too close, right here, my apartment. I'm not driving by, not going on to the next part of my day. Mark's voice is barely identifiable though his heavy breathing echoes from the sergeant's radio.

"Suspect fled. I repeat suspect is at large." The disgust in his voice is clear.

A steady stream of officers file up my stairs. My apartment is now a crime scene. Does that technically make me homeless?

My chest rises and falls in a wild rhythm as adrenaline shrieks across my chest. The officer steps forward to steady me as I sway on the seat of Mark's car.

"Oh." It occurs to me that I'm going to lose the half of a burger I ate. My legs wobble, but I manage to make it to the bushes before vomiting. Hands on knees, I watch Mark approach through bleary eyes. My stomach heaves again, and then Mark's there, strong hand on my elbow. I moan as I straighten. He's soaked with sweat.

"Whelks!" The female officer turns. "Get this to

the hospital. Most likely it's what he injected in Bobby Orville." She grabs the empty syringe Mark is holding out and takes off.

He turns to me, "I couldn't find him. I'm so sorry, Steph. That would've been the end of it. He was right there!" He hisses through his teeth.

"Mark." I swallow hard, throat burning, "He was way ahead of you; it's not your fault."

He softens. "I just want you safe." He looks down at his hand where my bottle of Citrus Essence glimmers.

"He dropped this and the syringe. Why does he want your oils, Steph? What's up with this stuff?"

I shake my head. "I don't know. It's not like he couldn't get his own." My thoughts tunnel, voice rising until I'm wailing. "Just go to essentialsense. com and click 'become a member,' enter number 11008146, then add your info! At least then I'd know your name!" I cry.

"Whoa," Mark says gently. "Here, does this stuff help with times like this?" Mark offers me the Citrus Essence. I nod, unscrewing it. I tip the bottle and wait for what seems like an eternity. Nothing.

"Come on!" I have to have some. I wrench the plastic dispenser off the top of the bottle, and it comes off with a pop and a blast of scent. Jamming the bottle against my palm, I hope a drop will come out. Something plunks against my palm.

I pull the bottle away, and there, in the puddle of oil, glimmers what I can only assume is a diamond.

Mark grabs my hand, leaning in as he too peers at the diamond. "Wow . . ."

CHAPTER SEVEN

WEDNESDAY, 6:17 P.M.

I watch Bugle sleeping peacefully at my feet on the floor of the police station. My body longs to join her, but the cramped meeting room is swirling with people. Everyone grows still as two men enter that I don't know. On their chests the white letters "FBI" stand out.

"I'm Mike Watkins, director of the Jewelry and Gem Theft Program. I'd like to see all the tapes you have on the perpetrator. This is Greg Fisher; he's our gems specialist. I understand you have the recovered diamond in your evidence room?"

Mark shakes Mike's hand. "Yes, sir. Jimmy's been compiling all the tapes."

He turns. "Sam, get the diamond from evidence."

He sweeps his arm toward the desk, offering it to Mike and Greg. "Go ahead and set up. We're dealing with the McMurray theft in Raleigh two months ago, right?"

Mike shrugs, "We'll know once Greg's had a chance to inspect the stone." He eyes the roomful of people. Mark catches his hint and snaps his fingers.

"All right, clear out." The room feels bigger with just four people and a dog. Mike turns to me. He's a thin wiry guy with close-cut salt-and-pepper hair, all business.

"I understand you're Stephanie Pierce," he says. "Ordinarily, you would be under arrest for having these goods in your possession." He stares hard at me and my mouth goes dry.

I nod, forcing my voice to work. "Yes, sir." Marks eyes grow hard as Watkin's words hang in the air.

"But you seem to be caught in the middle of a master thief's lifework."

I can't think of anything logical to say. "Oh" just doesn't seem to cut it.

The door swings open, and Dave pushes a cart through it with a small box on top containing the diamond and my Citrus Essence bottle. Soon, Greg has the stone under his stereo microscope and is reading off numbers to Mike.

"Every stone that's been inspected by the Gemological Institute of America is marked with a serial number. Ninety-five percent of the McMurray heist had serial numbers." Mike scans his list as he talks then heaves a deep breath. "In answer to your question, Officer Wellborn, yes. We're closing in on the McMurray thief."

A keen light enters his eye before he starts peppering me with questions. "Miss Pierce, you recently worked for Blue Stone Enterprises. Is that correct?"

"Yes, sir," I respond.

"And your position there?"

"I was CEO Harry Thorn's executive assistant."

"How long have you held that position?"

"Almost four years." It had been too long.

"And was all your work here in Raleigh?"

"No, sir. We travelled to Utah every two weeks. We spent two weeks working in Salt Lake City."

"Just what I thought," he says cryptically as he begins scanning his phone.

Greg beats them to the info, reading from his screen, "Two years ago, Miami Florida heist, $900,000 of cut gems stolen without a trace. Three months later, a female body found in Arizona with the smallest diamond that had been stolen taped to her throat." Mike grunts nodding, as Greg continues. "The woman traveled frequently from Florida to Arizona for work."

I shrink in my seat, and Mark steps to my side, towering protectively over me.

Mike says, "Antwerp, six months before that."

Greg chews his lower lip, then studies the list of stolen diamonds. "Three carats, VV S1. Excellent deep cut diamond, DF for color." He whistles. "Only number fifty and number twenty-eight on the list surpass this one for value. The question is, how many did he already fence in Utah?" Greg seems to be talking to himself.

Fence in Utah? What?

At the look of confusion on my face, Greg explains, "Fence is a word for selling stolen goods or even a person who acts as a middleman for selling stolen goods."

Mike turns to me again. "I understand you've had things misplaced for a while, Miss Pierce. Can you tell me how long?"

I scrunch up my eyebrows trying to remember. "Maybe five weeks?" I guess.

"Only in Raleigh or in Utah too?"

"Only here," I say then hesitate. "But no. No, that's not true. My purse lining got ripped in Utah the last time, and I'm still not sure how it happened."

Mike looks over at Greg. "Same MO."

I shake my head; all these acronyms are driving me crazy. "I'm sorry, but I don't get it. Why would there be a diamond in my essential oil bottle?"

Greg and Mike look at each other. Something is decided without words, and Mike turns back to me. "We believe Pete Payne has been using you to transport his stolen gems to fence to a black-market diamond buyer in Utah. He's the grandson of the infamous diamond thief, Doris Payne. He's on our most-wanted list with more than $100 million of stolen diamonds to his name both here and abroad. He disappeared from all social detection at age three. That puts him at age twenty-six. As a child, he was reported missing by his mother, but we believe his grandmother took him and groomed him to be her protégé. At any rate, her skill as a diamond thief certainly passed to him. We have no photos or medical records beyond his third year. As Greg said, he used the same plan two years ago. It didn't end up well for the woman he chose then. If I understand matters correctly, the situation has escalated rather rapidly in this case."

Mark jumps in, "The murder of Richard Hubbler was, as far as we can tell, his first mistake. Most likely Richard caught him entering Stephanie's apartment and confronted him. Stephanie later set up a surveillance camera in her apartment, or we wouldn't have had any clue that he was entering regularly."

I gasp loudly, making all three men jump, and Bugle roll up to look at me, head cocked. "I quit! I quit my job today." Seems as if that confrontation was three years ago. "I'm not useful anymore! That's why he broke in today. Somehow, he knew I wouldn't be traveling anymore. And he wants his stash back!"

Mike nods with a glint in his eye. "The question is, did he get what he was looking for?"

I respond bitterly. "He took all my oil except what's in my purse and that bottle of Citrus Essence."

I freeze. Do I have a diamond in my purse? I dig through its contents and grab the lavender and Relax I had at work, my mouth hanging open.

"The lavender was backward at work. I asked Harry if he was messing around at my desk. I even checked the cleaner's schedule." Unable to process it all, I look up at Mark.

He moves to the garbage can and pulls out a Styrofoam cup. "Here, let's dump it and find out."

I frown at the thought. It's one of my last oils, but I suppose I'll just pour it back into the bottle after we check.

I pop out the lid insert, and the crisp, peaceful scent of lavender fills the room. It's half full, so I tilt it slowly over the cup. Beautiful clear oil flows. Mike and Greg lean close, then back, blinking hard.

"What is that stuff?" Greg questions. I don't answer, tipping the bottle fully upside down. Plunk. We all jump at the tiny sound. Mike, Greg, Mark and I crowd the cup, peering in.

"What in the world?" Mike says. A swirl of smoke rises from the Styrofoam cup as it twists and curls up, even though no one touches it. The cup is melting, the oil is eating it away until the lavender runs over the desktop.

"Guess that's why they say to use stainless steel," I mutter, mourning the loss. But there in the center of the puddle sits another diamond.

"No," I whisper.

"Can I touch it, or will it eat my skin?" Greg questions.

"No, it's good for you. I guess it just doesn't like Styrofoam. Don't get it in your eyes," I warn.

Mark adds, "Or on your lips."

I glance at him, remembering the peppermint.

"You just remember my plan," he says under his breath, and I smile and nod.

Greg scowls through his microscope, reading off more serial numbers.

Mike's sharp bark of delighted laughter startles me. "Number fifty on the list! Got two of his biggest back! Empty the other bottle."

Mark digs further through his trashcan, comes up with a plastic cup. "Maybe this one will work better," he says.

"I hope so," I say as I tilt the bottle.

"I like that one," Mike says as the Relax's vanilla kick fills the room.

"You should buy a kit; they're popular," I respond, as the last drop of Relax comes out. No diamond. Everyone inspects the tiny bottle, and Mike clearly disobeys my warning by rubbing his eye after having stuck his finger in the bottle as far as it would go.

"You shouldn't have done that," Mark says. "It will be on fire in a minute."

I roll my eyes, bumping him with my hip while the two men stand talking with each other. He grins at me as Mike's eyes start to tear up.

"I did tell you not to get it in your eye," I say as I pour the oil carefully back into its bottle. I tuck it back in my purse.

Greg objects, "We are going to need that bottle for evidence." I've had my Relax now, so I stare him down, speaking slowly.

"No. Way. It's. Mine."

His eyes widen as he backpedals. "Well, I guess, since it was empty, but we are keeping this one." He slides the empty lavender bottle to his side of the desk.

Mike's next words make my blood run cold. "This is the closest we've ever been to catching this guy. We need bait. He doesn't know we found diamond fifty. We can put a fake in its place, and then Stephanie can lure him into the open."

"No," Mark's voice carries a steel edge. Their eyes meet, and I can almost feel the tension between them.

Mike gives way, shrugging. "Either way, we need a few days to plan and set up, which means Miss Pierce needs to be somewhere safe. We've got witness protection, WITSEC for short, available in Alabama and Colorado right now—if you'll agree to testify against Pete Payne at trial, that is."

I nod. "Obviously I will." I feel as if I'm under arrest. Just to test the boundaries more than anything else, I ask, "What about a conference in Dallas, Texas?"

"What?" Mike asks.

"Could I go to a business training by Dani Johnson in Dallas, Texas, instead?"

"Is it on your calendar?" he asks.

I shake my head. "No."

"Do you study her courses a lot? Have you spoken on the phone about it? Would he have any idea you would be going there?"

"No. It's sort of for oils, and I had thought I would be in Utah during the conference."

He grunts, considering. "I'll have an officer with you all the time, and you will wear a location bracelet." So, I am under arrest—sort of.

"Fine," I say.

"First, we need to know how many oil bottles you had. Can you find out?" I nod at Mike, logging into my Essential Sense virtual office.

"Oh," I say to no one in particular. "There's a little pink star by my name. I'm a Sapphire!" The men stare at me blankly. Never mind. I scroll down to the premium starter kit. "Okay, I had thirteen oils to begin with. No that's not right. I had fourteen. Sheena gave me another bottle of Relax." I read off a list of starter kit oils as Greg scribbles wildly to keep up. I add the extra bottle of Relax from Sheena to the end of the list.

"We've checked three bottles. The police combed her apartment and found nothing. We're running on two assumptions. One, Pete Payne took the rest of them. Two, the bottles were the only place where he had hidden the diamonds. Speaking of which, may I see your purse?" Greg asked.

I hand it over, but not before removing the Relax, my wallet and phone. He's crafty, that one. Greg inspects the tear in the lining of my grey Gucci bag.

"Umm. It's not torn; the seam was cut carefully." He takes out his jeweler's loupe. "Plus, there is a different stitch and thread here along the tear. He definitely hid some diamonds in here at some point. We'll have to keep this purse for evidence." I nod. See, that's why I kept my Relax.

A female officer sticks her head into the room, "Wellborn, you said you wanted word on Orville as soon as it came."

He stands up, "Yes, how is he?"

She smiles, "He will be just fine, thanks to you. If you hadn't recovered the syringe, they would have had no clue how to help him."

"What was he injected with?" Mark questions.

"Coastal Taipan venom. It is considered one of the deadliest snakes in the world—almost immediate paralysis, respiratory dysfunction, kidney issues, and at its end stages, cardiac arrest. He received antivenom within two hours of injection, so his outlook is excellent. Still a long road to recovery, but all things considered, he's in great shape." She nods, then steps out.

Mark releases a deep sigh. The news is a bright spot on a dark day.

THURSDAY, 5:45 A.M.

I spent the night in jail. Thankfully, it was solitary confinement. Five forty-five rolls around, and Mark is leading me out for coffee and breakfast.

"Did you sleep?" he questions.

"Actually, I did. I was exhausted; your knock woke me." I wipe the sleep from my eyes, wishing I looked a little nicer.

"Sorry," he says. In the light of the morning, everything seems better, even though I know it's not. Still, the small talk feels good. Normal.

"How about you?" I ask, as he opens the door to the outside world.

"Didn't sleep a wink. I was trying to think of a way to keep Mike Watkins from using you as bait. And researching Pete Payne. Found some interesting stuff. I read most of his grandmother, Doris Payne's, memoir." He nods. "I agree that she groomed her grandson to follow in her footsteps." Mark's patrol car is parked at the base of the steps. Bugle is wiggling like crazy in the back seat. I rush to open the door for her.

"Baby! Oh, I missed you." I cuddle her in the crisp cool of the early morning air.

I straighten. "Coffee. I need coffee." Mark opens my door after getting Bugle back in. Soon our bellies are full, and I'm fully caffeinated.

Mark checks his watch. "Should have just enough time to grab a shower if you like." I'm going to Dani Johnson's First Steps to Success with a police escort, compliments of WITSEC, and my flight leaves in about three hours.

"That would be great, but I thought my apartment was under quarantine."

Mark smiles at my misuse of the term. "At my place," he says, and my eyes widen.

"Ooohh. Then most definitely." Fifteen minutes later, we pull up at a lovely brick with a chain-link fence around the backyard and a huge pecan tree for shade.

"Wow," I say as he pulls into the driveway and parks. "It's beautiful!"

"Thanks. I've been happy here. We have to hurry though."

The first thing I notice is Bugle's bed lying on his floor. "How did you manage to get Bugle's bed out of the lockdown?" I question.

He laughs. "I didn't; I just bought her the same kind you had for her. I thought it would make her feel more at home last night. Apparently, it worked. She curled up on it all night while I paced."

Bugle settles in now as if it's been home forever. Maybe it's a sign. I watch Mark toss his keys on the counter. He's breaking down all my walls. What's the use of trying to resist him?

"Here." He hands me a bag, and I peer inside to see shampoo, conditioner, body wash.

I look up at him. "How did you know what kind I use? Your crazy research skills?"

"I just sniffed till I found the one that smelled like you."

That's it. I'm done resisting. I walk into him, forcing him back against the counter, drop the bag, and let my hands travel slowly up the small of his back around his ribs and up to his chest. "You are the most amazing person I've ever met." I reach up and pull his head down. Tilt my face to his. Ever so slowly my lips find his. "You taste good," I whisper.

A slow smile curls one side of his mouth.

Letting all my pent-up emotions go, I kiss him as well as I know how, which apparently is good enough. His strong arms draw me closer as I kiss his jawline, feel the pulse jumping in his thick neck.

A knock at the door makes me jump, Bugle barks, and Mark pulls me close, whispering, "Just when my plan was finally starting to work out . . ." I laugh low, and he continues, "It's Beck; she's going with you."

My mouth hangs open in shock. "Are you serious? How did you manage that?" I give him no time to answer before I kiss him again.

"It wasn't easy, honey," he says when I finally let him go. There is a pounding at the door; it's Beck for sure. I groan, snatching the bag of soap off the floor.

"I'm going to get in the shower. If she sees me now, she'll know I've been kissing you," I say as I head down the hall where he points me.

Mark grins, teeth white. "That wouldn't be so bad, would it?"

CHAPTER EIGHT

"All right, spill," I say, glancing up at Sarah, my U.S. Marshal bodyguard.

"I want to be a two percenter," she says. Dani had coined the phrase, and we have learned a lot the last few days. "My current salary is $55,000 a year; I'm putting my life on the line every day, and I'm ready for a change." Her blonde bangs almost covering her light-brown eyes need a trim. "What do you all do? 'Cause I need a passive income!"

I answer, my mind running over the revelations I've had. "We just got started with Essential Sense. We do essential oils, and we have every product you need to live a life free of chemicals. Their business structure is the best in the world." I smile. I can do this.

"Is that the stuff you gave me on Friday?" she asks. Sarah had been really under the weather on the plane, but she's just fine now.

Beck adds, "That was Germ Sniper oil and Respiratory."

Sarah nods. "I need more of that."

Beck eyes the firm muscular arms of my protector. "They have protein shakes and amino acids too."

I look at Beck, thinking about Dani's teaching on personality: the ruby, a leader; the sapphire, a full-of-fun person; the pearl, the one who cares for people; and the emerald, the one who does things by the rules. Beck is a total sapphire personality. Considering that I seem to be an emerald ruby, it's amazing we get along. Four basic groups—four ways to connect with people. I'm longing for even a short phone call with my ruby-sapphire Mark. But no calls, no credit cards—just me, Sarah, Beck, and a big wad of cash that WITSEC plan provided.

Sheena walks over, all smiles. "I'm so glad you all came this weekend." I shake my head; she has no idea. "So, what have you learned?" she asks.

It's too deep to say aloud, but Dani's story of overcoming abuse, fear, and depression spoke to me. It was the word I needed at exactly the right moment and showed me a different way of thinking.

Beck is the first to respond. "Oh, man! Where to begin? Bust out of my daily grind of average and move toward goals is the most important thing, I think."

"This is my ninth time at a First Steps to Success, and I still come out so on fire to grow and make a difference in the world," Sheena replied.

Sarah interjects, "Well, I need to get started in a business that I can grow in! I plan to come back to the next conference in six weeks. I feel as if I've got so much mindset changing to do, it will be all new next time."

"Well, Steph can get you in with Essential Sense; it's been my freedom. I quit my nine-to-five two years ago, and I've never looked back." Shenna's story is encouraging.

I sigh, thinking back to my own real life. I had quit too. The crazy swirl of events and danger seemed so far away the last three days. I needed this time to be in another world where things are normal—almost—aside from absolutely no contact with anyone. Plus, I don't see the point of the dinosaur of a phone they had given me as I'm not allowed to call anyone anyway.

Sarah's eyes never stop scanning the crowd, and she's always within three feet of me if we're not in our hotel room. Still, I feel alive and energized. Changed. Of course, that could be the three packs of Superberry I've been drinking every day.

Sarah looks at her watch. "We need to head down; our cab should be here in five minutes to take us to the airport."

Bugle. Mark. I can't wait. Stalker. Shoot. Determination to get him out of my life rises.

"Let's go." Sarah buys a premium starter kit while we sit at the airport. Then Beck and I put our heads together and start looking into the life of Doris Payne.

"Did you know she started stealing diamonds to get back at whites? She felt they were the reason she grew up in poverty." Beck is deep in Doris's history, enthralled with her unexpected story.

"Nope. Look, this article says both her children were raised by their father in another state. She tried to reconnect with her daughter during her teen years, but the girl wanted nothing to do with her."

"It's a sad story altogether isn't it? I can see why after a life of taking everything she wanted, she would snatch her grandson too. Can you imagine growing up like he did? Could he be anywhere near normal?" I shake my head at her question.

"He isn't normal. But he is smart. Does any of this information tip us off to his next move?" Beck sighs.

"Not that I can see. I certainly don't see anything about oils in her life."

A few hours later, I step off the plane, and there's Bugle right at the landing gate, one giant wiggle, and the most gorgeous man in the world holding the leash.

"Lucky bum," Beck whispers to me, and I can't help grinning. Yeah, it all has been worth it to have gained what's in front of me.

Mark's shoulders drop in relief when he sees me. He releases a deep breath. Three days did feel like forever. I kneel with Bugle circling and whining happily in my arms as Sarah shakes Mark's hand.

"She's all yours now," she says, totally not knowing how right she is. Then she's gone down the congested hallway.

I look up at Mark. I shiver as his eyes say it all. You're all mine now.

A slow smile spreads across my face. "Hi."

He juts his chin in my direction. "That was a long weekend." His deep voice betrays him, full of emotion. We walk out of the airport with Bugle sniffing everyone. Beck hails a cab and takes off while we load my suitcase in the back of Mark's patrol car. We get in; Mark gets tired of looking for a break in traffic, so he flicks on his blue light. A cute smile plays on his mouth. "Love that," he says as we cruise quickly out of the airport.

Soon he pulls into a parking lot, puts it in park, and flicks his radio. "ETA twenty minutes." His dark eyes scan my face, and warmth spreads up from my belly. "When I get this chest camera off, I'm going to say hello properly."

I arch one brow teasingly. "Yum."

"You all right?" he questions.

I nod. "Yeah. It was good. Really good. I needed a few days to put myself back together on the inside."

"You're beautiful inside and out," he says.

I lean forward and whisper, "Get rid of the camera."

Mark smirks then grows serious. "So, I was hoping that Pete Payne got what he wanted and was going to move on to another city, another robbery, and just leave you alone."

For the first time, I don't crumble inside at the suggestion that he didn't. "But he won't. What happened?"

"Your place in Utah was broken into." Mark looks at me sideways, "He also tried to clear out your bank account."

I grip his arm claw-like. "Tried to?" I question.

Mark nods. "And failed. As soon as you entered WITSEC, all your personal accounts were locked. Pesky little fellow is getting desperate." I let out a breath of relief. Mark arches one brow at me. "You're worth a lot of cash."

"Yeah. I had a plan too," I say. "Pay cash for a house and own my car outright by the time I'm thirty. Not nearly as fun as your plan though."

"Beat you," he says.

"What do you mean?"

"I'm twenty-five." He squints at me. "That's not too old for you, is it?"

I think of his intense speed as he took down the naked guy. Nope, not too old. "Wouldn't change it for the world." Besides, Beck had told me his age long ago.

He keeps going. "Good, anyway I beat you to buying a house for cash, but mine is a truck—not a car. It is all mine, though."

I punch him in the arm; my fist looks tiny as it connects.

An expression of horror crosses his face. "Don't hit an officer of the law, or I'll have to arrest you."

I roll my eyes. "So, Mister 'I've Got It All Together,' what's the plan for me? Am I going to be bait?"

His hands squeeze the steering wheel hard, threatening to twist it out of shape. "That's what we're going to find out. The feds have more say than I do right now. Sadly."

We merge back into traffic and soon arrive at the station. Bugle stands in the backseat stretching. It reminds me of the first time I ever came here.

"You know the day you told me to come here before work? You messaged me to bring Bugle too. I will never forget you in your glamour pose, hip against the desk, head thrown back—laughing."

He laughs now. "Glamour pose?"

I nod. "This one," I say, crossing my arms high on my chest and pushing out my ribs.

His brows go up. "You like that one, do you?"

I can see the wheels in his head turning. "Yeah, but first, I need not to be stalked by a thief."

He deflates. "My plans will all come together one day."

It's all I can do to step out of the car away from Mark's bubble of happiness and safety and not even hold his hand as I lead Bugle back into the station.

MONDAY, 10:45 A.M.

Mike and Greg face off against Mark and two other officers, arguing about a plan that's turning my stomach. It seems crystal clear to me that Mike has only one goal: to catch Pete Payne at any cost, including my safety.

My head follows the increasingly tense conversation back and forth as if I'm watching a ping-pong match. Suddenly, the building shudders, dust rises from the walls, and the sound hits my chest, leaving my ears ringing.

Bugle leaps straight up from the floor, and Mark's swept me off my chair in a heartbeat. He's rolled us to the floor and is covering my body with his. The other two are down on one knee, guns sweeping over Mark and me.

Maybe it's just my way of surviving, maybe I'm getting used to crazy things like this, but the only thing I can think of is Mark's body hovering over mine, his elbows near my ears. I hadn't thought this far; he is so huge. I can't wipe a goofy smile off my face. Bugle army-crawls next to me, trembling. Poor baby.

Mark's head is turned as he shouts orders at the top of his lungs. The veins in his neck stand out. I'm completely mesmerized in my own little world where there is only Mark Wellborn and me.

"Now!" Mark shouts, and suddenly he's somehow scooped me off the floor in a roll, and I end up over his shoulder like a sack of potatoes. He jets down the hall, one hand holding me in place, pistol in the opposite hand. The other officers follow, guns scanning. We turn into another room, and Mark flips me onto my feet in a corner of the windowless area.

He's huffing; I'm no featherweight. Bugle forces her way in behind me. My ridiculous grin grows. I think I am in love.

Mark's radio crackles as he turns, gun steady. "Explosives to a silver Honda Accord, no perp on tape. Most likely remote detonation." Is that my super-calm operator from the day I found Richard?

Mark hisses under his breath, turns back to me. "I'm moving you to a more secure room. You ready? Or do you want me to carry you?"

"Whatever you say, Jedi Master." He looks at me frowning; I shrug. "You can carry me. It will be faster." More fun too. Before I can blink, he's scooped me up again. Bugle is behind, running full out. A giggle wells up, stuttered by the concussion of my stomach against his shoulder. How in the world can he move this fast?

We repeat the huddling in the corner; but this time, since I'm behind him, and there's no chest cam to catch me, my fingers run up his ribs.

"Woman, you are something else," he says over his shoulder. His radio crackles, the sound tripled by those of the two other officers standing in the doorway.

"Building clear. No current threat. I repeat, no current threat." Mark releases a long breath, his gun holstered now.

"Come on." He pulls me up from crouching in the corner. "Let's go find Mike. Things have shifted in our favor. The feds can't use you with deadly intent on the table."

I nod. "Right. Come on, Bugle. It's all right, baby." She shakes off the stress. It seems as if she shakes it right onto me. Without touching Mark, I'm back in the real world—where my car just got blown up.

A few minutes later, I'm staring at a slow-motion replay. Just off the center of the screen, my car sits sandwiched in the parking lot. Then there's a flash. My silver Accord shoots into the air, flames boiling under it. Cars on either side flip away, crashing into the next ones. My beautiful car tilts to the right, rolling hard before it smashes down two cars away from its original blackened space. It burns and burns, flames licking skyward.

"My favorite sunglasses were in there."

MONDAY, 8:59 P.M.

Mark walks down the hall toward me. He looks as tired as I feel. "Ms. Pierce," he says, "would you please come sign some papers in my office?" His smile is so sweet as he stands in the doorway, arms across his chest.

He pumps one eyebrow. "Glamour pose, right?"

I lift bleary eyes, "Oh, I noticed, no worries." My body complains as I stand up. It's been a long, long day. The station has been crowded with extra-duty officers due to the attack on police grounds.

"You seem much happier than you did an hour ago when you left." I glance up at him questioningly.

"Yes, ma'am, the paperwork for you to sign will pull you out of Mike Watkin's hands and straight into mine."

I look at him sideways. "Finally," I smirk. But that smirk claims all the extra energy I have. In no time at all, I've scribbled my name on a domestic violence protection order against Pete Payne.

"We're going to move you to the Southside station for tonight. They've got a luxury suite over there." He shrugs. "Relatively speaking. Plus, if we plan well enough, he won't know we've moved you. So, all in all, you can get a good night's sleep."

"I never thought I would look forward to sleeping in jail, but all things considered, it sounds pretty good. Safe." I say, thinking of my car exploding on police grounds. "Mostly. What about Bugle? Where will she stay?"

Mark looks down at me. "I'll take her home with me after you're settled," he says.

I nod, thankful that Mark's pulled all his favors and gotten her to stay with me this long. I look up at him, "Thanks. You're my hero."

He frowns, "Some hero I am. If I had my way, I would've kept you in WITSEC until Pete Payne was in jail or the ground. Mike's got a screw loose, willing to catch him at any cost. Your cost." His square finger taps the paper I just signed. "But this takes you out from under Federal law and puts you back under North Carolina state law."

He holds out his hand, "Come on, let's go to jail."

Mark had arrived in front of my cell at 6:45 a.m. with one of my favorite work outfits. I raise my brow: shoes, sheer pantyhose, my chambray necklace. I finish emptying the bag. There's even another purse with my funky WITSEC phone and an oil roller with "Go get 'em" written in Beck's handwriting on the label.

"We've got a 7:30 appointment with the sheriff. Bugle wouldn't be allowed there, so I dropped her off with Beck, hence the makeup and the oil. I had already gotten the outfit. She asked if I had clothes for you, and I said 'Yeah, I got everything she needs.' She put her hand on her hip and said, 'You're either smart and brave or dumb and stupid.'" He laughs as he hands me a Starbucks Grande Double Cream and a toasted bagel.

"You're smart and brave for sure." He hadn't missed a thing. I step inside his still full hands, ignoring the chest cam, hugging his neck. He wraps me in a careful coffee hug.

"Beck is a nut, isn't she?" I say. The scent of the coffee makes me happy. "What would I do without you, Mark Wellborn? You thought of everything." Tears burn my eyes as I hang on, soaking him up.

A deep sound rumbles in his chest. He looks down at me, "I've been looking for you for years, Stephanie Pierce." Our eyes lock, and something deep, almost spiritual, transfers between us.

"I'm glad you found me," I say.

"You'd better get changed. We can't be late," he says.

Walking out of the tiny lime-green bathroom, I feel well put together. Pretty.

"How did you get my favorite outfit? How'd you know?" I sip my coffee, tucking the roller bottle into the super cute pocket in my skirt as we exit the building. I try to pretend that there aren't three patrol cars waiting or four officers scanning our surroundings carefully. Mark's car sits in the middle; we get in before he answers.

"Well, I stood there in your 'quarantined' closet . . ." All three patrol cars pull out together; I feel like the president. "And I thought to myself, if I was the kind of person who had to have her toothbrush aligned just so next to the sink, how would I keep my clothes? Probably from best to worst. And since you're a smart woman, I figured you'd probably put the best on the left just the way you start a sentence. And, voilà, the first skirt's tag was all worn out and the last one on the right was still stiff and new. Since you keep your clothes in sections in the closet, I repeated the procedure for a shirt and shoes."

I grin behind my hot cup. I smile as I say, "That's creepy."

He hooks the car around a corner, "I've been a policeman a long time. Studying people is an essential skill. You, Miss Pierce, are the most captivating subject I have ever encountered."

It must be the heat from the coffee making my cheeks warm.

At 7:28, my team of five bodyguards escort me into the Sheriff's office in formation. I shake Sheriff Steve Toler's hand.

"Ma'am, it seems as if you've been through quite a lot lately. Today we're going to nail down a plan to get you safely back to civilian life."

I dip my head. "Thank you."

Mike and Greg file in, and soon we're in an intense study of Pete Payne. Mike Watkins stands in the front of the room, a laser pointer in his hand as he runs through a PowerPoint. "On June 5 at 7 a.m., a security alert sounded at McMurray's Jewelers. The security guard had opened the vault at the normal time only to find it nearly empty. It's one of the largest jewelers in the state, and the only one with a three-foot thick concrete vault two stories underground.

"But Pete Payne didn't start his heist there. First, he broke into a low-security apartment above Maria's Pizza next door. Sliding a thin sheet of aluminum over the window alarm, he disabled it quickly. From there it was a quick walk to the delivery area that connects the four shops in the rear of the buildings on Pen Avenue. Even though McMurray's didn't use the delivery area any longer, an old door with an updated security system still connected it to the warehouse.

"We believe he'd been working at Maria's for quite a while and was familiar with the area. The door was easy to defeat, but right inside was an infrared heat sensor. Easing the door open, Payne slowly placed a homemade polyester quilt over the sensor. It displaced his body heat and gave him a chance to move past it toward the security station. Two guards later swore they heard nothing. Next, he descended into the vault's anti-chamber, using the elevator maintenance shaft. Inside the shaft sat a combination motion and heat detector. He carefully sprayed a thick layer of hairspray over the sensor. This was his weakest link, as there was no way for him to know how long the hairspray would confuse the sensor. Now it was a race against the clock; he was in and had to get out as quickly as possible.

"After descending the shaft, he somehow squeezed through a vent at the bottom that was no bigger than a hole in a cinderblock. Pulling his duffel bag behind him, he then entered the blackness of the antechamber. He slipped heavy contractor garbage bags over the light sensors and then flipped on the lights.

"He stood looking up at the vault door. First thing, he withdrew a precut slab of aluminum, and with heavy-duty double-sided tape, he stuck it to the thick magnetic plates on the vault doors. If they separated at all, an alarm would sound. Then with the aluminum holding the plates together, he unbolted them and slid them over to the wall and screwed them into place. Here's why we believe Payne had at least one accomplice. There is no physical way he could have suspended the weight of the magnets while he fastened them to the wall." Mike shrugs.

"Next he opened a small service box in the ceiling and carefully stripped the wires until the copper showed. Then he clipped a precut wire from the outbound to the inbound cables. The system was now a loop, and from that point, none of his activities inside the vault could be recorded. No impulses could jump his wire, and he was free and clear of security except for the vault combination itself. We later found one tiny camera affixed to the fire extinguisher top. Somehow he had accessed the vault at least once previously and placed the camera so all he had to do was watch his footage to get the combination."

Mike's hand comes up, his fingers flicking, "Poof. One million in diamonds gone. The vault rarely had that much loot, but a safe in South Carolina was undergoing an update, and its contents had been added to the McMurray vault. I have to admit I'm impressed; Payne is good at what he does.

"And as for the car he blew up yesterday . . . no trace whatsoever on the surveillance cams of his having tampered with it. So, it's probable that he had it rigged for weeks or even months."

I shiver. Mark reaches over for my hand and squeezes it.

My phone vibrates. I reach into my purse searching for it, pushing aside the Relax. It's only when I'm looking at the screen that I realize nobody has this number. I don't even know it.

My thumb trembles as I click the new text alert. Vomit rises in my throat; I force it back down. A picture of Bugle smiling her goofy smile, her curl sticking up in the middle of her head is bright on my screen. In the foreground is a gun pointed straight at her forehead. I put my hand over my mouth as sweat breaks out.

The phone vibrates again with a text message. "Tell anyone and she dies."

I lean back in my chair, keeping the screen from anyone else's view.

Buzz. "Go to the bathroom."

I look up at Mark seated beside me, leaning forward with his elbows on his knees, intent on the update. Can I do this to him?

The vibration makes me jump. "Now." The picture of Bugle is still on the screen.

Can I live with myself if I don't try to save her? I stand up, trying not to wobble, trying not to think. "I have to go to the bathroom," I whisper, avoiding Mark's eye contact. He snaps his fingers, gaining the attention of the female officer with Branton on her name tag. I'm fighting just to stay upright, my heart tugging me forward as we exit the room.

"Bathroom is to the left," she says.

I nod, not trusting my voice. Branton stops outside the door, and I go in.

The phone vibrates. "Go into the third stall. Climb up on the toilet, then flush it. Immediately swing open the vent above you. Do it quickly. In order. Or Bugle dies."

My shoes slip on the back of the lid as I bend down to flush it. The vent creaks as it swings down, perfectly muffled by the sound of the commode flushing.

Buzz. "Climb."

Tears start to roll as I reach up for the grate's edges. Somehow, I scramble up.

Buzz. "Turn left, crawl twenty paces on the structural beam."

I bite my tongue to force away the tears, letting my anger rise. You can't crawl a pace anyway, Pete Payne. That's only for walking. There isn't even a word for what you're making me do.

Buzz. "Open the grate. Drop down onto the boxes and exit the door on the right."

The boxes crumple under me and cups explode out of their sides as I muffle a squeal, hitting the ground. The bright light of the morning is harsh through the doorway as I open it.

Buzz. "Turn right, jog to the end of the building."

How does he know where I am? I reach the end of the building.

Buzz. "Walk to Pearl Street and turn right."

My mind races. How do I know he'll let Bugle go and not have both of us? I text as I walk. "Let her go."

"Shut up."

"No!" I stop walking. "Text me a picture of her loose."

Seconds tick by.

"Text me a picture of her loose." I send it again.

"Keep walking."

I turn around.

"I'll shoot her."

"You'll never get your diamonds," I respond. I bite my lip so hard I taste blood.

"Walk to Fourth Street, and I'll let her go."

Well, it's something at least. I force my legs toward Fourth. Just shy of the sign, I stop again.

Buzz. Bugle's blonde tail is high. She's trotting away from the photographer with no leash—free and clear. I scour the picture, zoom in on the street sign. It's Pearl and Fifth!

I look up. There in the distance, I see her trotting away from me on the sidewalk. I open my mouth to call her, but something stings my hip.

"Ahh!" As I whip around, my hand finds a syringe still stuck in my hip.

"Oh." I keep turning. A shadow looms over me. "Jerome?" I question . . . right before the world goes dark.

TUESDAY, 5:56 P.M.

I blink up at the Jerome with green eyes. We're in a basement. I'm tied to a hard metal chair; the single lightbulb above my head flickers.

"You seem to be missing a bottle of oil, Steph," Jerome says, his voice silky smooth.

My mouth feels as if it's full of cotton balls, and my eyes burn. The thoughts in my head swirl like soup. Why does Jerome have green eyes? Did I fall and hit my head?

"It's a bottle of frankincense, Steph."

I swallow hard. My stomach twists, and I fight the vomit back down. Suddenly I have to have water. "Water . . ." I croak.

"No, Steph. Oil." Jerome's acting super-calm, almost as if he's high.

I try to remember what I could have done to make him tie me to a chair. "I'm sorry I got shampoo in your eyes." At least that's what I meant to say, but nothing comes out clearly.

"Get Leann, will you?" I try again.

Suddenly he's in my face, close, forcing my eyelid open.

"Ugh." I turn my head to the side, resisting his touch. I pay for the fast motion as the room spins.

Jerome purses his lips. "Not awake yet, Steph? I'll be back in a while." Then he flicks off the light and disappears. The darkness is total. My mama's words float back to me from when I was a child. "If you're afraid of the dark, honey, just close your eyes and tell yourself to believe that it's light outside and that your eyes are just closed, sweetie."

"Okay, Mom. I love you. Good night," I respond. Reality and time are a swirl of confusion. I squish my eyes shut tighter. Trying to sort out how old I am proves to be too hard. I take in a deep breath, and for a second, my head is clearer. My name must be Steph; that's what he called me. How can I know Jerome's name but not my own? Somewhere deep down there's a pulsing sensation that things are not all right. Then my eyes snap open in the pitch black of the basement.

Memories like waves crashing on the shore pound me. Bugle, Harry. Oh! Richard. Don't let the tears start. Don't. Mark Wellborn, his chest dripping blood, entranced with me. The diamond in my hand. Oils. My car exploding, Bugle running away down the busy street. Don't get hit, baby! Jerome with green eyes. Not Jerome—Pete Payne! My skin crawls with the revelation.

What easier way to know my schedule than to work at doggie daycare? I see the black-and-white surveillance video in my mind, the hooded man and Bugle jumping at him—just like she did every day. A high-pitched moan escapes me. She just wanted to jump into his arms. How stupid, Steph! How could you miss it?

Desperately, I yank at the ropes tight around my wrists and ankles. The chair cuts into my wrists as I struggle; its metal legs screech on the concrete floor. I grip the armrests hard. Ouch. Something pricks my finger. I force my wrist forward, sawing the rope against the sharp point. My skin burns, but I won't stop. In the dark of the basement I hear the rope fibers snapping. Come on!

The rope loosens, and I work it faster. The door creaks open, and I freeze. Do something! Only one hand is free! The light turns on, and I grip the arm-rests with both hands. My heart pounds as Jerome descends. I stare at the floor as Jerome stops in front of me. All I can see in my mind is the picture of Bugle with a gun pointed at her head. Anger boils up, and I raise my eyes.

"Give me the oil, Steph," he orders.

Before I can think, my loose fist flies toward Jerome. So hard in fact my chair tilts forward, and the chair and I together take Jerome down.

"What?" Jerome is on his feet in a split second, but the chair keeps going, and I twist my wrist hard trying to keep from landing on my face. The oil roller falls out of my skirt pocket, the glass crunching under the armrest. A blast of lemon and herbs rushes up at me. Still tied to the chair by one hand and my ankles, I'm stuck. Still, I force my free hand into the oil. The chair rocks, and Jerome grunts as he flips my chair back over. I come up swinging. From this angle, I swat at his face, and oil splats across his eyes.

"Argh!" Jerome reels back as the chair settles upright. "Should have seen that coming!" He wipes his eyes with his sleeve, then leaps for my free hand, smashing it against the chair. In a second, I'm tied tight again.

"It burns! Oh, it's worse than the shampoo." He turns, fumbles his way up the stairs and turns out the light. Now there is too much time to wonder what he will do when he comes back down.

The lights flick on, and I clench my eyes shut against the searing brightness. Pete Payne trots down the old wooden staircase. The trembling starts in my legs and spreads to my arms. I force myself to meet his gaze. His eyes are red, lids swollen. What had possessed me?

"Didn't expect you to do that, Steph," He shrugs. "Gran is a spirited woman too, so . . ." he pauses, deciding. "I will have to keep a better eye on you. I was getting a bit frustrated. You lost my oil bottle, Steph. I want it back."

I stare up at him, building a wall between us in my mind.

"Tell me where it is, Steph, or I'm going to have to hurt you, Steph." He's driving me crazy saying my name like that. I look hard into his intensely green eyes. His pupils aren't dilated, but it sure seems as if he's on something. I need to start playing his game, then outsmart him. Right, the guy who slipped off with a million in diamonds under the noses of security guards. I nod. Yep, that's what I'm going to do.

"Okay, what kind of oil was it?" I resist adding his name at the end.

"I already told you, Steph. Frankincense."

I nod, "Of course, it's the best one; of course, that's it." Didn't he already steal all my oils? How am I supposed to know where it is?

"Yes, Steph, it's my favorite oil. So peaceful, so clear. Not at all like your favorite, Steph, Relax. Can't stand it, Steph; you smell like it now." His mocha skin wrinkles on his nose in disgust.

"Well, soon you'll have your frankincense back," I say.

"Tell me where it is, Steph. Right now." His voice has suddenly lost its light and wispy tone. Now it sounds like steel.

The shift is not okay. Pete Payne's got a screw loose, and I'm at his mercy.

"I'm way behind schedule. I want the oil bottle now."

I wish I could wipe the sweat from my upper lip. "I am pretty sure you took it from my apartment."

Payne's fists crash into the metal armrests of my chair, his face right in mine, spit flying as he shouts at me. "It was the only one missing, Steph! The only one I really wanted. The only one I filled! Tell me where it is!" he snarls. The veins in his neck stand out. He shakes my chair hard, making my teeth rattle. The metal chair flexes as my head snaps back and forth.

Breathing hard, I try to keep my voice quiet. "I'm trying to remember." He growls in response, shoving my chair back hard across the floor. I strain against the motion, willing it not to tip over.

"My syringes will help you remember, Steph." He turns toward the stairs.

I can't let him get whatever drug he wants to inject me with. Come on, Steph! Think, if he didn't find it in your apartment, then where is it? My gut turns. I'm missing something; it hovers in my mind just out of sight. "Wait! Wait, I know where it is!"

Payne turns halfway up the stairs. Mom's friend, Cindy, has it! I hope. Somehow, I've got to play this to my favor. I've got to get out of this basement. "Give me a phone, and I'll get it for you." I try to control my tone to match Jerome's silky smooth one.

"You think I'm an idiot, Steph? Just tell me where it is." He trots down the stairs.

"No, you're incredibly intelligent. But there's one problem: Mark Wellborn has it. That's what I did with it; I gave it to him." If I tell Pete Payne where the frankincense really is, he'll leave me here tied to this . . . I shut off the thought. What else can I tell him? All the movies I've seen swirl in my mind. He won't have time during a trade to open it to see if it's the right one. Any bottle of frankincense will do. Beck's bottle. I just have to get a message to Mark.

"It's highly unfortunate that you met him. Even more unfortunate that you were the one to find Richard's body. It was my first mistake. First one." He shakes his head, mourning the past. "What does Mark have to do with it?"

A flash of inspiration sparks in my mind. "I asked him to put it in a safe deposit box at PNC Bank." I can almost see the wheels turning in Payne's head. A safe-deposit break-in would take weeks to plan and pull off. Run with it. "If you let me call Mark, he'll bring it to you. Then you'll be back at square one, ready to set off with your plans. Mark's in love with me. He'll do anything I ask; just let me talk to him." I hold my breath. Payne is starting to crack; his foot taps nervously. It's not a good sign for me.

"You pulled off the most incredible heist of the century; you can think of a safe way to trade me for the frankincense." For a second, he looks like the young Jerome I knew. He nods; minutes pass. Let him think, Steph. I bite my tongue to keep nervous words inside.

Payne blinks, slides a smartphone out of his back pocket. "No words about me, Steph, no extra talk. You tell him to bring the frankincense. He'll get another call for the location tomorrow at noon." He presses the phone to my ear. How does he know Mark's cell phone number? I shiver.

"Hello?" I hear Mark's voice.

"Mark," I say his name, and my throat threatens to shut tight. "Do you remember the bottle of frankincense I gave you when we met? Remember my mom, Cindy Pierce?" My mom's name is not Cindy. "I told you to put it in your safe deposit box at the bank, remember?"

"Are you all right?" Mark questions. Payne's hand grips my upper arm like a vice. I wince and ignore Mark's question.

"Be ready to trade it for me at noon tomorrow."

Payne yanks the phone away from my ear, throws it to the floor and smashes it into bits with his heel. There's another needle in his gloved hand.

THURSDAY, 11:58 P.M.

Fog rolls through my brain, swirls of confusion. I seem to be stuck in a backbend. Did I fall asleep this twisted up? My stomach aches from the stretch, and a cold, dirty floor presses against my face. Which way is up? I open my eyes. The world looks as if it's tilted and swirling.

My wrists are tied to my ankles behind my back. A spit-soaked gag is too tight around my head, and it has effectively sucked all the moisture out of my mouth. Pushing my mind, I wonder what the last real thing I remember is . . . Jerome. Needle in hand.

Sweat breaks out as I think. I'd flipped my chair, desperate to keep him from injecting me; that's why my head hurts.

Wormlike I buck, twisting, trying to see something other than the peeling paint on the wall. Feet. Jerome's. Sweat drips down my back. I twist my eyes up his long figure as he checks his phone and then squats down next to me. My lungs pump hard, dragging air through my nose.

"It's time. Listen now. Don't forget anything, Steph." He's back in his super-calm, too controlled mood. His awful bloodshot eyes remind me of shampoo.

"You're wearing an insulin pump over your heart. I control it remotely."

I search my chest, willing my skin to feel if it's there but I can't.

"What I loaded it with will kill you in ten minutes if I release it." He pauses. "Obedience. That's what I need from you. I can reach you from anywhere. You'll be good for me, won't you, Steph?"

I nod, muscles screaming from being tied.

"That's why I picked you. You're so predictable, so nice. I'll miss you, Steph."

I think of the woman in Arizona and shiver.

"Here's what's going to happen, Steph. The ketamine I gave you can mess with your head. Just in case you don't remember, I wrote you a note, so you won't make mistakes. Mark's going to bring the bottle of frank. See the red square of tape on the floor? Here?" Jerome points to a small square of tape on the floor halfway between the door and the window.

"He's going to put the bottle right in the middle of it. And then he's going to untie you. Every cop is going to exit the building. I will know when it's empty. I will know if you've been obedient, Steph. If it's the right bottle, I won't press the button that will release the venom into your heart, Steph. Don't mess with the Omni port either. Don't bump it. I made it really sensitive just for you, and if you try to peel it off, it will inject you. Goodbye, Steph."

He places a typewritten note on the floor by my face with his gloved hand and then a phone. He sets his finger over the green button and pushes it. Then he's gone.

The phone rings on speaker. Only once, then I hear the most wonderful sound. "Stephanie?" Mark's voice is intense.

I bite the gag hard, spit dripping down the side of my face. "Huummuh." Stupid Jerome.

"Stephanie, are you alright?" The ketamine fog is starting to clear, rolling out of my head.

"Come get me," I respond, but it comes out as "Kana et mmm." A tear of frustration drips along with the spit. Come get me, Mark.

"I've got the bottle of frankincense. Can you tell me where you are? Steph?" I thrash my head. The gag is too tight, and it feels as if the edges of my lips are cut.

"Mmhmm." For some reason, my mumbling makes me think of the first time I met Mark, and the words wouldn't come out right in his presence. I laugh through the gag, and everything is suddenly clear. The person I was then was so small—so stuck in such a tiny world with no hope.

I lift my eyes to the peeling paint of the ceiling. What I see now, instead of fear, is life. And for the first time when I think of the future, it's without fear. Tied in an abandoned building with venom taped to my heart, I suddenly feel freer than I ever have. I'm an Essential Sense business builder. I'm going to marry the most handsome man in the world. I'm going to live, love, and have babies.

"We're going to make a trade, right? You for the frankincense." Mark keeps talking, trying to make a connection.

"Yes, just put it in the square of red tape and take me away." But of course, he can't understand a word.

I imagine a technician frantically tracing the location of the call. Mark is getting in his car now. I can hear the door shut with almost no noise at all, but my hyper-alert senses are picking up everything—the dampness of the floor, the screaming tightness of being hogtied.

"Do you have any instructions?" he asks.

"Yshhhh, lshhht." Yes, Mark, I have a list. Carefully, I twist and do my best inchworm impression keeping my right shoulder still, so I don't bump the insulin pump. There's the door, the hallway leading to freedom. Minutes creep by.

Mark has gone silent. I start listening for sounds in the building. I jerk at an almost imperceptible scuff in the hallway. Then Mark steps into the open doorway, gun steady, scanning. I take as deep a breath as I can through my nose. He's here. All in black, he and his team enter, fanning out and covering all the exits.

Mark holsters his gun and slides to one knee behind me. There's the snap of a knife opening and then the nerves in my arms rebel against the motion as he saws at the thick strap around my wrists. Ping. I curl forward for the first time in hours.

"Aaahh!" I cry. There's nothing but my body screaming out at me in pain and every muscle cramped. My hands flush red after hours of no blood. Mark is working on the cable tie at my ankles. Now the knot at the back of my head. The evil gag loosens, and I wince as blood trickles from the corners of my mouth. Mark's strong hands raise me to a sitting position.

"Ouch," I say, but all the pain fades as I look into his eyes. He's all business as his thumb gently pulls down my eyelids.

"He drugged me," I mumble through numb lips. Still, Mark doesn't respond. I slide my feelingless hand slowly toward the note. Mark snatches it up, jaw clenching in anger as he scans it. His eyes snap back to mine before he rips my shirt down over my left shoulder. A hiss escapes him. I peer down at my chest. A tiny medical device is indeed adhered over my heart.

Mark rips open the Velcro pocket in his vest and withdraws the bottle of frankincense.

"Is it Cindy's?" I question, knowing Jerome with green eyes will push the button over my heart if it's not. He nods, jaw tightening as he stares at the port. He scans the letter again and places the bottle carefully in the center of the square of red tape. He drags his hand back along the floor. A tiny square of black plastic emerges from under his palm. My eyes find his in question. He nods again: it's a camera. The note goes into his breast pocket, and suddenly I'm in his arms.

The other cops fan out, some ahead, some behind, as he carries me through the tight doorway. I wrap my tingling, sluggish arms around his neck. Staring up at him, breathing in his scent, determination wells up in my heart. I'm going to live. I won't live in fear either. I'm going to live for real.

Mark tucks me through another doorway and down a flight of stairs. Maybe it's the ketamine, maybe it's the intense thankfulness I have to be alive at this moment; either way, right now, floating along in Mark's strong arms, I only know one thing. I don't want Jerome in my life anymore. But the undeniable truth is he's medically adhered over my heart.

A sheen of sweat covers Mark's face as we bunch up in the main doorway. Guns point outward in every direction. A black van comes to an abrupt halt in front of our door, and its extra-wide side door slides open.

Mark nods at the officer to his left, signals to the men. I curl up tight in his arms and somehow, we fit through the van door. Mark spins, crouched, finding a seat. He still holds me, as two escorts file in, the door clicks shut, and the van surges forward.

An EMT crouches in front of us. "She's got an insulin pump loaded with who knows what over her heart." Mark's voice is gravelly, as he takes the type-written note of his pocket. The thin EMT's eyes scan it quickly.

He erupts in expletives, then pulls my shirt down off my shoulder, clicks on a powerful mini-penlight, and struggles for balance as we turn a corner. He continues to examine the area over my heart. Chewing his upper lip, he shines a light on the pump. "It's an Omni port, properly installed." He shakes his head. "Can't risk trying to remove it; I've no idea what he's done to it."

"Can it be remotely activated?" Mark asks, a twinge of desperation in his voice.

"Yes, an app on any phone would do it—not sure at the distance though. They will know more at the hospital." The flashlight burns my eyes as he pulls down my lower lid.

"Patient is in stable condition, no major injuries visible." His fingers press my wrist, counting heartbeats.

I look up to find Mark searching my face. Our eyes meet, and tears well up in his eyes. His fiancée Leah and now all this with me. A will made of steel rises from my heart. I'm done being under Pete Payne's thumb. The paramedic lets go of my wrist. I peer down at the evil Omi port. Lord, help me.

Before I can think, before anyone can object, my hand flashes to my chest. My fingernails rake deep into my skin, scratching the Omni port clean off my body.

Beep-Beep. Sitting in my hand like an overturned turtle, a tiny jet of liquid squirts up into the air and falls onto my palm. I look up at Mark, a twinkle in my eye. "I got it."

His horrified expression gives way as he laughs in relief. "Woman! You are something!"

I wish I could smile, but my lips are too sore. The EMT with gloved hands is bagging the Omni port as evidence, and as carefully as we can, we scoop the tiny amount of liquid from my palm into a vial. I stare at Mark as the EMT wipes my hand down with an alcohol swab.

Fighting off tears, I ask, "Did you find Bugle?" My free hand clutches his vest.

"Yeah, she's safe. A deputy picked her up on Pearl and 18th." I melt in his arms. Thank You, God.

"How did Jerome get her? She was with Beck, right? Is Beck all right?" I pepper Mark with questions. He smooths a stray lock of hair behind my ear as he responds.

"She took Bugle for a walk. She said a man wearing a hoodie came up behind her and pushed her down, snatched her purse and Bugle and ran. Her phone was in her purse, which I'm certain Pete knew, so she couldn't call. He must have had a car parked nearby. By the time she got back to her house, got in her car and drove here to the station, you were already committing your traitorous act of following Pete Payne's directions." He says this last part gently, but I still shrink inside.

"He had a gun pointed at Bugle's head. I couldn't do anything else." I drop my eyes at my poor defense.

Mark gently lifts my chin till my eyes meet his. "Just keep me in the loop next time, all right?"

I nod. "I'm sorry."

He shakes his head. "She's your baby; I get it."

I change the subject. "Did you and my mom have trouble figuring out my clue?"

"I wish I'd met your mom under better circumstances. I knew her name wasn't Cindy the second you said that. So I called her, and she took us right to Cindy's house who, thankfully, had been unsure what to do with the oil, so she had stuck it in her cabinet." His brows go up theatrically, "That bottle was loaded."

I nod. "He said it was the only one he filled."

Mark continues as the paramedic wraps a blood pressure cuff around my upper arm. "Ain't no way Mike Watkins was going to let those diamonds go.

But thankfully, he had a line on fakes that matched perfectly. We spiked the Frank with blacklight reactive powder and diamond number twenty-eight's replacement with a nano tracking chip." He looks down at me, half his gorgeous mouth tipped up, "He wasn't counting on you going kamikaze, risking ripping off that pump though, was he?"

I take Mark's compliment, wishing I could smile. That was the bravest thing I've ever done. "I decided I was going to do it while you carried me out of the building. Couldn't stand the thought of him touching me while I was in your arms." I flatten my mouth, disgusted. "Plus, he called me predictable."

Mark laughs again.

The paramedic is after the blood crusting at the corners of my mouth with a cotton swab.

"I got it," Mark says, snatching the swab out of his hand.

"Uh, no, it's my job."

Mark says nothing in response, just pins the EMT with a rock-solid gaze.

"Right," the EMT says as he retreats to the front of the van. Mark grunts in satisfaction.

Oh, I could just eat him up.

"Here now, got to get these lips all better; my plan won't hold off much longer."

I feel a familiar red flush creeping up my neck as he works on my lips. I can tell the second he notices because a smirk plays at the side of his mouth. Soon enough though, the exhaustion rolls through my body. I rest my head against Mark's chest, and the steady beat of his heart lulls me to sleep.

I watch my mom fuss with the oils Beck had brought to the station. Every muscle screams as I shift on the closed toilet seat. Being hogtied was tougher on my body than I could have imagined.

"Put the copaiba in there too, will you, Mom?"

She nods, finishing the six drops of lavender and Soothe, then adding copaiba.

I had just stepped out of another jail shower; with Jerome still at large, I don't have any interest in going out into the world.

Mom hugs me again. She just can't stop.

"I'm fine, Mom, really, just sore. Your prayers paid off."

She holds me at arm's length, studying my face. Frowning at my bruised cheeks, she says, "It's a good thing you already had that handsome detective wrapped around your finger. He was a force to be reckoned with coming after you. I knew he was in love with you the second he shook my hand. The two of you will make beautiful grandbabies."

My face flames red, "MOM!"

Beck steps into the tiny bathroom, saving me from my mother's predictions. Bugle squeezes in too, whacking everything with her tail. Beck is as quiet as I've ever seen her.

"Beck, there's no use feeling bad that Pete stole Bugle from you. It's not your fault; he had it planned perfectly. I'm the one who's sorry you got dragged into this." She doesn't respond, and that's not a good sign. Got to get her talking. "How's your bottom, anyway?"

Beck's mouth tips up. "Well, strangely enough, since he pushed me into a fire hydrant, I have a bruise in the shape of a smiley face on it. I guess I hit the bolts just right. Want to see it?" There's light in her eyes again.

"Well, yes," I say as she half-moons my mom and me.

"Wow!" Mom and I say in unison. "It does look like a smiley face." I hold out some of my oil mix.

"Thanks." She smiles.

"Here, honey, we'll go out, and you can slather your front with this, and then I'll rub it into your back."

"Thanks, Mom."

I stare into the mirror after they leave. My cheeks are bruised a deep purple from the gag, and I can't open my mouth without cracking open the corners. But strangely, it's my eyes that catch my attention. I should be broken, afraid, traumatized, but the woman staring back at me is confident and strong. Free. God, thank You. Thank You for keeping me even in the valley of the shadow of death. Thank You for Mark Wellborn. Thank You for Bugle. Thank You for essential oils.

I open my eyes and look at my chest—at the angry red patch of skin where the adhesive tape was, at the tiny red dot where the Omni port's needle had been under my skin, and at the four red, raised slashes where my fingernails had dug in deep. I had done that. I'd done what needed to be done without hesitation, without research, without planning. I pull my super-soft shirt down over my shoulder. I look at the oil bottles my mom has left on the green sink. One faces this way, the other label that way. I nod; it's just fine. They are perfectly all right like that.

THURSDAY, 10:03 A.M.

"It's gone!" The female officer named Martinez is staring at the tiny camera's live feed and shouting. "I didn't even see him take it!"

The screen splits, and she replays the last thirty seconds. The bottle of frankincense is there and then, blink, it's gone! No hand reaches out for it; nothing else moves. A huge screen flicks on as the room begins to fill with people. Mike and Greg straighten from slouching in their chairs, and Sheriff Toler stands in front of the screen, arms crossed.

"Martinez, pull up the chest cams." A few seconds later the screen splits into a view of three different officers' chest cams: Mark Wellborn, Jim Thompson, and Dave West. Their names scroll in white letters under the bottom of their part of the screen.

147

"He's moving. Still in the building, but the sensors are moving." She clicks her screen and a 3-D scan of the building I'd been tied up in rotates; we're now looking at a side view. The little red blip drops straight down to the ground floor.

IT Officer Martinez presses her headset tight against her ear as she relays the info to Mark and his team. "Perp is ground level, southeast corner of the structure." The chest cams turn in unison, and the early morning light makes even the dilapidated building bright.

Martinez's fingers type wildly. "Lost the signal." She shakes her head in frustration. "Fan out! I have no signal, Wellborn. He could be anywhere."

Did he know that they're fakes and leave the diamonds and transmitter? I swallow hard at the thought of his being free in the world. We watch as the three chest cams show quick movement surrounding the building. The minutes of searching turn into hours as the helicopters circle, and police swarm the area.

By the time Mark returns to the station, I'm worn out. I hand him a pack of Superberry, and we drink them together. "You don't seem as concerned as I thought you would be," I say, watching as he tilts the packet up high for the last drop.

"That's because I have a plan." He looks at me and says, "This stuff is good."

"Yup. So, this must be a different plan than the one I'm familiar with." I blow air into my Superberry packet, then tilt it up for the last drop. Ouch.

"Remember I said I read Doris Payne's memoir? Pete's grandmother?" he asks.

"Yeah, you said you found some interesting stuff." I resist nodding so I won't hurt more.

"She's the key. Did you know she's still alive?" I frown at this info. I'd Googled her too after talking with Mike.

"Didn't she steal stuff in the sixties?"

Mark nods, "Yeah, she's 87 now. Got busted last year for lifting $86 worth of stuff from Walmart."

"Really?" I say, not quite believing it.

"She started stealing when she was 17 to provide for her mom. Then it became a game to get back at the whites for treating her as if she were nothing. Gem theft became a thrill for her—the only thing that made life worth living. She studied style; she would spend weeks getting an outfit together that made everyone believe she was blue-veined. Doris Payne was a master at sleight-of-hand. She always went into the jewelry stores with a large ring of her own. She'd get the clerk deep in conversation, and all the while she would be switching rings from finger to finger. Once the clerk had lost track of all the rings she had tried on, she'd slip an extra under her own piece and walk out. It would be hours before the clerk had to admit he couldn't locate a ring in the inventory.

"In her late twenties she met a fence who would change everything for her. His name was Babe, an ex-baseball player and a playboy too, into anything dirty, with high connections that kept them both out of prison on multiple occasions. He eventually became her lover too. He died ten years later, and it was the start of a downward turn for Doris. He seems to be one of the few people she really loved. Even her own two kids were raised by their father in another state. I have a hunch that she took Jerome and raised him, trying to make up for the years she spent loving no one."

Mark pauses for a moment as I process all that he's told me. Then he goes on, "I look like Babe. I'm going to pay Doris Payne a visit with some gems in hand. She was living homeless on the streets last year in Georgia. She's not much better off now. She can't resist diamonds, never has been able to. Babe always got her out of trouble, and I'm going to step in and show her some of Pete's loot, tell her he is going down unless she convinces him to turn himself in. She'd done it at least five times with Babe and gotten off Scot-free. She will contact him. We have her phone tapped; then we'll know exactly where he is. That's when I'll nab him."

I stare at Mark, impressed. "It's a good plan," I say.

"Yeah, even Mike thinks so. I'm gonna need a suit though. Style. It's what got her into all the high-class stores so she could swipe their gems. She's a sucker for style."

"I got you covered. I have inside connections at Nowell's. It's the only place Harry would get fitted around here. Jack's the best." Dressing Mark will be fun.

Mark looks like a movie star. Armani suit, tight in all the right places. "You're keeping that suit, right?" I say as I watch him packing his bag, tucking a pistol in the bottom.

"You like it?" he asks.

I clear my throat. "Yes."

"It's time to go. Kiss me, woman," he says, grinning. I frown, wishing my mouth was healed up. I smooth the soft fabric of his vest over his muscle.

"It's all right. I got this." He nibbles my neck instead. Then he's looking deep into my eyes. "Stay here in the station with Bugle while I'm gone. My return flight is in three hours. No matter what, don't leave here without me. Okay?"

"I will. Be careful, will you?" I say, fighting fear.

He snorts, "She's 87. I'll be fine."

"I know. See you soon."

FRIDAY, 12:30 P.M.

"Come on, you old broad," Mike mutters as we watch the screens. Mark's mission had gone according to plan, and Doris Payne has diamonds in her hands again for the first time in years. He was certain he had rattled her with Pete's current situation.

Martinez tucks her chair in tighter, pressing her earpiece against her head. "Outbound call from Doris

Payne's number." I hold my breath. Martinez has five screens open as she types furiously, triangulating the location of the phone receiving the call.

"Hello?" a female voice answers.

I deflate; it's not Jerome.

"Tell him to contact me the way we talked about." Click.

"Got it!" Martinez shouts. She clicks Mark's screen and gives him the address. He'd driven down to the south side of town almost as soon as he'd changed into his swat gear. His hunch has been right too; he's parked in an unmarked car only minutes from the address.

"The phone she called is moving south on Vine. Slow, most likely on foot."

Mark's voice is grainy over the radio minutes later. "WF, pink jacket, shorts, dark hair, entering 115 Vine." Martinez clicks from screen to screen.

"Yes, that was her. Outbound call from her number."

We wait, listening.

"One twenty-five," is all she says, then hangs up.

"Triangulating." Martinez informs us. "Call to two blocks north of your current location."

And so it goes, four more two-second calls, Mark and his team following the addresses.

"Inbound call to Doris Payne!" Martinez almost jumps off her swivel chair. "Fifty-eight East Church Street. Your ETA should be two minutes."

My heart starts to pound.

"Gran?" Jerome's voice sounds from the screen.

"Boy, you in trouble," Doris's voice wobbles with age.

"I got things here, Gran. I'll see you in a week." Click.

Go, Mark, go! We watch the map screen; five red dots are closing in on the new blue dot that is Jerome's phone. Martinez brings up the chest cams on the main screen, split into thirds again. Mark exits his car, crouched low, heading toward a two-story brick house. Sam and Jim appear on the far side of the structure, guns low. Is the blue dot moving? Martinez zooms in on the map. "Suspect moving through the house, east side. One exit on that side of the building."

Mark creeps around the front corner, well-muscled forearms holding his pistol steady. Martinez catches Jerome's move first.

"Heading north toward Pine. Move!"

I breathe out. God, keep Mark and be a shield to him, Lord.

The chest cams show three pistols steady in a double-handed grip out front. Mark leads, sprinting to the rear corner of the building.

"Rear exit. Suspect is moving toward the underbrush on the east side of the building."

Martinez clicks a third screen and up pops a map of the area. "Entering a concrete drainage ditch, left turn, he'll go into a tunnel. Right turn; he'll be into the clear."

Jerome's blue blip begins to move again. "Suspect is in the ditch, turning left toward the tunnel. Lights ready."

Mark turns the corner, crouched but moving fast. The other two officers fan out behind him, and I watch Sam's screen as Mark's explosive speed pulls him ahead. Overgrown bushes obscure the yard, and Mark and the others switch on their pistols' flashlights.

I grip the chair in front of me, white-knuckled. Jerome is fast, but Mark is gaining on him. Jerome looks over his shoulder, then puts his head down and stretches out, running for his life.

I watch Mark in Sam's screen; his arms are pumping missile-like as he barrels toward Jerome. The third officer is even farther behind, offering yet another view. Jerome disappears into the dark mouth of the tunnel. Don't go in, Mark! Just let him go. My hands cover my mouth. He crosses the barrier of darkness, and his camera flips to infrared.

"Suspect three feet from your right hand, incoming!" Mark spins in the dark, the beam from his gun's light too small to catch Jerome, who looks like a demon in the black-red-and white infrared. Just before reaching Mark, he twists hard, his right foot swinging up toward Mark's hand. Mark's screen blinks dark; he must've ducked. His hands flash up in the infrared. Empty. It seems like slow-motion as Mark's red and white fist connects hard with Jerome's stomach. He flies back then slides across the ground, rolling up to run back at Mark. I imagine the darkness, the listening, heart pumping.

Sam's flashlight beam sweeps into the tunnel, confusing the camera, and our screens flash from infrared to darkness. I lean forward. Where!?

In Sam's screen, I see Jerome crouched low and catlike, closing in on Sam, but just outside of his light. A heartbeat passes.

Martinez shouts, "Sam, incoming!" But her warning is too late.

"Sam's down. Wellborn, 2 o'clock!" Mark spins, but Jerome's infrared outline is already there. Sam's camera is black, and Mark's shows only a mass of red, white, yellow, as they fight.

Jerome slides on his back again, limp for a moment. Jim enters the tunnel, confusing the cameras again. Then there's nothing, nothing in the tunnel but darkness. I look up at the top screen: Jerome's blue blip is moving fast.

"Run! Straight ahead, suspect has exited the tunnel." The bright end of the tunnel grows as Mark closes in on it. Jerome's dot turns right, then stops.

"Suspect twenty yards, east side. Possible hidden vehicle." Mark speeds up, then breaks into the light. Martinez powers on another screen with a bird's-eye view from a helicopter rushing toward the scene.

"Four paces," Martinez warns as Jerome explodes from behind a concrete piling. My eyes find his right hand; a syringe flashes in his fist.

"No!" I shout, making everyone jump as Jerome sweeps out with the needle. Mark leaps, avoiding the jab, but Jerome has already spun, his fist barreling again. The camera jumps. It's too much movement to catch what's happening. Jim exits the tunnel, and then I have a clear view of the fight. Jerome stabs again, but Mark snatches his wrist.

Instantly Jerome twists hard, his foot flying for Mark's head, but Mark yanks Jerome's wrist and sweeps out with his right foot kicking Jerome's weight-bearing leg out from under him. Mark follows him to the ground, pinning him. Jim's camera closes in, and I watch two screens full of the green-eyed Jerome's angry face.

He thrashes hard, his empty hand coming free of Mark's grip for just a second. I watch in horror as Jerome bites down hard on his own wrist. Now there's something in his mouth, red and blue. He sneers up at Mark as he starts to chew. Foam wells up and begins to drip out the sides of his mouth. He begins to convulse. His eyes roll up in his head, and a blue tinge creeps out from the corners of his mouth. He bucks violently then goes still, his head lolling to the side. Suddenly he looks like the Jerome I knew. Young and likable. Jim reaches in, searching for a pulse.

"Suspect is dead. I repeat, suspect is dead," Jim huffs through his radio.

TWO WEEKS LATER, 11:30 A.M.

I wander into my bathroom. I stare at my sink; my toothbrush is flipped over. A shiver runs down my arms until I see a note lying underneath.

Mark's tight perfectly aligned script says, I knew you would notice right off. Find number two in your closet. A smile steals across my face as I run to my room. Digging around in my closet, I find another note tapped on a new shirt. Put it on; then you better make sure you smell good. I put on the shirt and then think, must be oils?

Heading to the kitchen, I finger the cracked tile where Bobby's gun had slammed into it when Jerome kicked it out of his hand. It had really happened, and I'm okay with it. I scan my oil shelf and find yet another note taped around a bottle. I peel it off and gasp. A bottle of Warm Glow sits in my hand. I read the note: Oh, yeah, baby. I laugh, Oh, yeah.

Treasure awaits. Find it where I hugged you tight. I read the ingredients of Warm Glow; I'd better use some carrier oil. I rub it on, thinking hard. We definitely hugged here at my place. And his. But then again, it had been more than just a hug. Kiwanis Park, after he pulled me over. He held me there and hugged me tight. I smile; that was the moment I fell in love with him. Really, really fell for him. I bite my lip in anticipation. What could it be?

"Come on, Bugle. Let's go for a walk." She jumps up, tail swinging. The drive is beautiful, especially in my new black Lexus. Bugle surges everywhere when I get her out, sniffing. I glance around, no truck, no patrol car. Hmm. Is this the right place? Will I find more directions?

I step out on the path that Mark and I had taken. Bugle pulls toward a bench on the right. Is that a little box sitting there? A smile overtakes me. I stand looking at it for a moment, searing this memory into my soul. I can't wait any longer, so I lift the lid and pull out a dark-blue velvet jewelry box. Treasure indeed. I slowly open it.

"Ah!" An intricately beautiful engagement ring glimmers inside.

A shadow shifts, and then Mark is there towering behind me, his solid chest at my back. I twist in his arms, a question in my eye.

"Marry me, Stephanie. Tell me you'll marry me."

I look into his eyes, my hero, my soulmate. I open my mouth, but before I can utter a word, he's kissing me with all the passion that I ever imagined a man could have, until I can't tell up from down. The more of him I get, the hungrier I am for him. Finally, he takes the ring and slides it on my finger. It's a perfect fit.

"So?" he whispers.

"Yes!" I breathe. "A million times, yes. I love you."

He grins that irresistible grin. "Recognize it?"

I stare down at my ring. "Recognize what?" I question.

"The diamond! It's number fifty—the one that was in your lavender bottle. Fought hard to get it too. After all, it was the diamonds that brought us together. And since you're going to be an Essential Sense diamond someday, I thought this one would be perfect for you."

I smile at his thoughtfulness.

I look up at him as he says, "You had me hook, line, and sinker the day your shoe got stuck in the staircase. But the day that we found number fifty, that was the day I knew it was forever."

DID YOU ENJOY THIS BOOK?

You would make my day if you would leave a review on Amazon with your honest opinion! Go to amazon.com/author/crfulton to leave a review. And don't keep this book to yourself! Would you share it with all your "oily friends?" Post a selfie of you and this book on your social media page and tag me in it! I would be thrilled to connect with you. You can also reach me at crfultonbooks.com.

AUTHOR'S NOTES

Want to know more about the true story of Doris Payne? Follow Beck's example and research her. She really did everything—except raise a grandson. Want to know more about Dani Johnson? Go to danijohnson.com and become a 2-percent person!

Do you need to relax? Are you looking for a peaceful place to work, or reconnect with family? You can find it at Intent Focus on YoutTube. Experience soothing piano music mixed with ocean waves, forest sounds, or just the incredible beauty of the instrument. This channel is great to listen to while reading my books! While I'm writing, my husband is often playing the keys, or composing new music. We are really good at teaming up after 17 years of marriage, let us help you unwind today.

Visit https://www.youtube.com/watch?v=6DnK-0KrCVs8 today and don't forget to subscribe for more great music!

— C. R. FULTON

COMING SOON...

Book 2: Villains

When Beck goes to visit her reclusive grandmother in Montana, something's clearly not right. A deep-seated fear grips the town of Riverbend, and messages in essential oil bottles heighten the mystery. Where will the trail lead? Can a city girl survive the wilds of Montana? Or will she need the help of a handsome Navy SEAL?

Book 3: Gunman

When Sydney Smith is framed for an assassination, it will take all her essential oils, wits, and the help of a mysterious man to keep her from falling even deeper into trouble. With the evidence stacked against her, she must prove her innocence before the clues are gone.

C.R. FULTON

Book 4: Spies

All Olivia Welsh wanted was a beach vacation and a relaxing cruise. What she got was double agents, crime scenes, and a man who just might steal her heart. Her stash of essential oils may only prove to cause a case of mistaken identity that leads to mayhem.

ADDITIONAL BOOKS BY C. R. FULTON

Swiftmain
978-1-949711-46-2
$18.95

Whispers in the dark. Vague clues. Deadly threats. As currents of unrest flow throughout the kingdom of Andrea, Raina Swiftmain holds knowledge that could save her people. But can she find the missing links and discover the location of the lost prince? Dare she trust a knight who claims to hold the answers she needs?

Ironhold
978-1-949711-61-5
$18.95

War is imminent. With only a handful of untrained men, Raina and Torin must find a way to protect the Prince of Andrea and muster an army. Will walking in faith be enough to change their lives for the better?